지뢰꽃 마을 대마리

Daemari, The Village of Landmine Flower

정춘근

1960년 강원도 철원에서 실향민(황해도 아버지와 평안도 어머니)의 아들로 태어났다. 1999년 『실천문학』에 「지뢰꽃」 등을 발표하면서 작품 활동을 시작했다. 시집으로 『지뢰꽃』, 『수류탄 고기잡이』, 『황해』, 『반국 노래자랑』 등이 있다. 현재 고향인 철원에서 글쓰기 지도 및 문맹 퇴치 봉사 운동을 하고 있다.

지뢰꽃 마을 대마리

Daemari, The Village of Landmine Flower

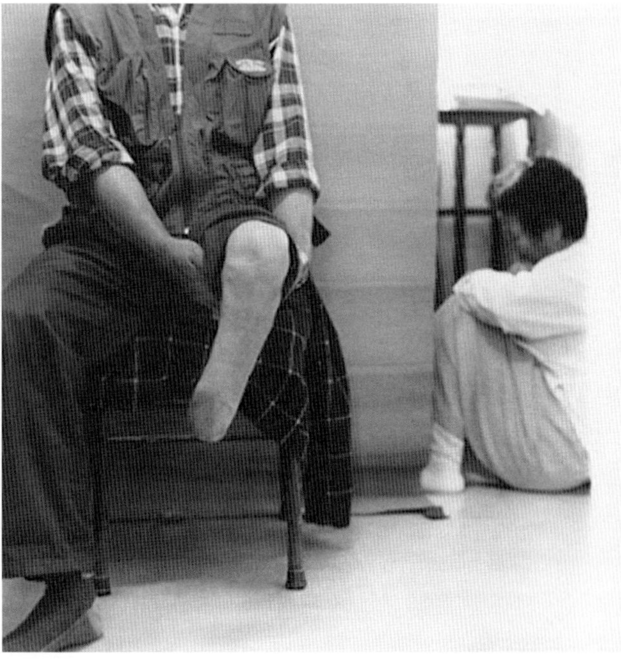

차례

발간사

이번 시집에는 DMZ 접경 대마리 마을 개척 역사를 담았습니다.

시의 주제는 한국 전쟁이 끝나고 버려진 땅을 농경지로 이용하기 위해 출신 성분이 좋은 150명을 선 발해서 군 부대장 지휘 아래 지뢰밭을 개간했던 이야기입니다. 북한군과 국군 사이에 있는 계곡에 텐트를 치고 직접 만든 탐지기로 지뢰를 제거하는 작업을 하면서 10%에 해당하는 사람들이 지뢰 사고를 현장에서 사망했습니다.

그렇게 목숨 걸고 개간한 곳은 나중에 땅 주인이 나타나서 빼앗기거나 돈을 주고 사야 했던 분단의 그늘 아래서 벌어졌던 숨겨진 아픈 역사입니다. 우리가 극복해야 할 분단은 이런 사람들의 눈물을 기억하고 닦아 주는 것에서 시작한다는 생각으로 시 작업을 했습니다.

대마리 개척 역사를 널리 알릴 생각을 하던 중에 서울대학교 김지나 박사를 비롯해 자유전공학부 학생들이 영어로 번역하는 작업에 적극 동참, 사려 깊은 지성과 뜨거운 열정이 더해져 볼품없는 글에 가치를 높여준 것에 감사를 드립니다.

또 시집 해설 부탁에 흔쾌히 승낙하신 이영춘 시인님과 출판 기회를 준 실천문학사에 감사드리며 마지막으로 이 시집을 대마리 개척 역사에 바칩니다.

2020년 만추에

정춘근

Preface

This anthology holds the history of the development of Daemari village on the border of the Demilitarized Zone between North and South Korea. The poems tell the story of 150 people, selected by the South Korean government for their "clean" political background, and tasked to clear minefields on land abandoned during the war in order to redevelop it into farmland. They set up tents in the valley between North and South Korean military forces, and cleared mines using tools made with their own hands. One out of every ten would perish while carrying out this task.

Yet even though they risked their lives for this land, later the "true" landowners would appear and take the land away, or the land would have to be purchased with money on top of the blood already paid. This is their painful history, hidden underneath the shadow of Korea's division. I wrote these poems with the thought that the path to our reunification must begin with remembering the tears these people shed, and wiping them away.

I thank Seoul National University's Student Program Coordinator Dr. Jina Kim and students from the College of Liberal Studies for raising the value of these humble works through their enthusiastic translation of these poems into English and addition of their intelligence and passion.

I thank poet Lee Young-chun for cheerfully accepting my request for writing a review for this anthology and Silcheon Munhaksa for giving me opportunity to publish.

Last of all, I dedicate this anthology to the history of Daemari's development.

From the autumn of 2020,
Jung Chun-geun

대마리 이야기 1
— 서른 마지기 소문

"땅 서른 마지기를 준단다."
"그것도 공짜로 나눠 준단다."

긴가민가한 소문이
수복 지구를 떠돌았다.

사방 공사에서 돌아 온 아재들은
허황된 헛소리라 수군수군
사문안천에 빨래 나온 아낙들은
뜬소문이라고 소곤소곤

또, 땅 사기꾼들이 지어낸 말
이북 놈들이 퍼트린 유언비어라며
돌고 돌았지만

수복 지구 사람들에게는
말짱 거짓말이라도
간만에 가져 보는 꿈이었다

Daemari 1

Rumor of Thirty-majigi

"They say they'll give you thirty-majigi of land"
"They say they'll give it for free too"

Dubious rumors
haunted the Re-taken Areas

Guys returning from erosion control work
grumbled it was all absurd nonsense
Wives doing laundry by the Samunancheon Stream
murmured it was all groundless gossip

Word went round and round
that land fraudsters made up the tale,
or commies from the North spread the myth

But for people of the Re-taken Area
though it may be a downright lie
it was a long-awaited dream

대마리2
— 사실로 확인된 소문

서른 마지기 소문이 사실이었다

읍사무소 김주사에게
막걸리 사주고
슬쩍 들은 이야기로는
대마리 벌판이란다

남한과 북한이 뻰질나게
총질을 해대는 사이에 버려진 땅
삼십 년도 넘게 자란 갈대
한가한 버드나무만 우거진 땅
가끔 고물 캐러 갔던 사람들이
끔찍한 사고를 당하는
자갈보다 지뢰가 더 많은 땅

인민군이 신탄리까지 내려와
막걸리를 먹고 들어가는 길목

처음에는 고개를 절래절래 흔들던 사람들이

눈만 감으면 아슴프레하게
떠오는 땅 서른 마지기에
그까짓 죽기야 하겠느냐
낡은 삽자루를 꽈악 잡아 본다

Daemari 2

Rumors Confirmed

The rumor of thirty-majigi was True

A drink of free makgeolli
for Kim in the town office
spun secret tales
of fields in Daemari

Land emptied in gunshots
between the south and the north
Land where reed grows thirty years tall
where idle willows grow thick
Land where junk pickers dare delve
and return sometimes terribly harmed
where more mines than pebbles hide

The corner where the People's Army
come down to Shintanri for makgeolli

People would shake their heads at first
but behind closed eyes
sway thirty-majigi of land

What more would one suffer than death?
They grasp the handles of old shovels

대마리3
— 연천 사람들

자네, 이야기 들었나
자네, 그 소문 들었나

대마리 개간은
연천 사람들만 자격이 있다는
말 같지 않은 소문
대마리는 분명 강원도 땅인데
경기도 사람들에게 넘겨준다는
기가 막힌 이야기
이미 연천 사람들이
개간을 시작했다는 소문
사람들은 귀를 의심하며
자기 땅을 빼앗긴 것처럼
억울한 심정이 된다

노인들 서넛 만 모이면 궁시렁
사방공사 나간 아재들도 투덜투덜
사람들 불만이 삐죽삐죽 터져 나와
주먹을 꼭 말아 쥐고

읍사무소로 찾아가고
군청으로 달려가는
큰일이 벌어지기 직전

철원 주민들도
참여한다는 이야기가 들렸다.

Daemari 3

Yeoncheon-gun People

Kim, have you heard the story
Lee, have you heard the news

The ridiculous news
that only Yeoncheon people have the right
for Daemari reclamation
The absurd story
that Daemari, doubtlessly the territory in Gangwon-do Province,
is to be handed over to Yeoncheon people, residents of Gyeonggi-do Province
The news
that Yeoncheon people already embarked on the reclamation
People felt bitter and resentful
as if their own lands are stolen
hardly believing their ears

Muttering from the old, every time they gathered
in groups of three or four
Grumbling as well from men at erosion control

work
Since grievances from people popped up with a pout
they were about to make a fist tightly
burst into the town hall
and dash for the district office
Just before making a scene

It was heard that
Cheorwon people, residents of Gangwon-do Province
were also going to take part in

대마리 4
—전략촌

대마리 개척단
이름은 전략촌이었다.

이북에서 온갖 폼을 잡고
지어 놓은 선전촌에 대응해서
우리가 더 잘 산다는 자랑을 하기 위해
만들어진 마을이었다

순찰을 하던 사단장이
황무지로 버려진 대마리를
평소에는 개간을 하다가
전투가 벌어지면 바로
총을 들고 나서 싸우는
이스라엘 기브츠 비슷한 구조를 만들면
땅도 얻고 전투력도 얻고
꿩 먹고 알 먹고 생각에
만들어진 전략촌이었다.

이런 계획을 모르는

수복지구 사람들은

누구나 갈 수 있다는

꿈에 부풀어

신청 받는 날짜만

손꼽아 기다리고 기다렸다.

Daemari 4

Strategy Town

Daemari pioneer team
the name was Strategy Town

The village was made
to respond propaganda villages
made by North with lots of efforts
to brag that we live better

While patrolled
the divisional commander thought
if in Daemari, the wilderness
on usual days, doing reclamation
on days with wars, promptly
fighting with guns
if making it similar structure with Israel Kibbutz
could get both land and fighting efficacy
could eat both pheasant and eggs
Daemari was a Strategy Town made for that thought

Not knowing this plan

people in re-taken areas
just looked forward to
the day of application
buoyed up by the dream that
anyone can live there

대마리 5
— 신청 조건

드디어 전략촌 입주 신청을
동송읍사무소
철원읍사무소에서
받는다는 소리가 들렸다

아무나 가는 것이 아니라
까다로운 조건이 붙어 있었다
여러 사람들 배알을
뒤집어 놓는 조건들이
울퉁불퉁 덕지덕지 붙어 있었다

군대를 제대한 사람
나이는 마흔 이하
식구는 네 명 이하
재산이 10만 원 넘어도 탈락
사상이 건전한 사람
행정 기관 추천 도장을 꽝 받아서
근엄한 선발위원회를 통과한 사람

이렇게 조건을 붙이고 보니
노인들은 갈 자격이 안 되고
이런저런 핑계로 군대 안 간 사람
식구가 많아도 안 되고
재산이 많아도 안 되고
까다로운 조건을 맞춘 사람들은
에라 모르겠다
서둘러 신청을 했다

Daemari 5

Application Condition

Finally it's told that
Application for moving to Strategy Town will be received
at the town hall in Dongsong-eup
Cheorwon-eup

Not for everyone
but for the qualified
Application details,
making people peeved
were posted
messily mussily

Man who finished his military duties
Man who is under 40
Man with less than 3 family members
Man with no more than 100000 won in hand
Man with obedient thought
Man who passed our honored selection committee
with recommendation from administrative agency

After posting these conditions
Application was not for the old
not for those who didn't serve for army
not for those with many family
not for the rich
Qualified people
without a second thought
applied in a hurry

대마리6
— 입주증

전략촌 입주 신청자 중에
빨간 물만 비쳐도
무조건 탈락을 시켰다

방첩대에서 가족부터
친척의 사돈에 팔촌까지 조사해서
고분고분 말 잘 들을 수 있는
사람들을 추리고
또 추려서 입주 대상자를 결정했다

입주증을 발급 받기 전에
기가 막힌 각서를 썼다
군부대 지시에 잘 따르고
개간하는 과정은 일급비밀
그리고 지뢰 사고로 죽이도 좋다는
요즘 말로 표현 하자면
신체 포기 각서를 썼다.

그리고 1년 동안

남자들만 가 입주를 해서
군부대 지휘를 받으며
지뢰밭을 개간하는 조건도 있었다

Daemari 6

Residence Permit

Among the applicants to live in Strategy Town
anyone who had the hint of red even just slightly
were disqualified immediately

The CIC investigated our family
and your relatives, close and distant
to sift and sift
for the meekest, most obedient people
who would get to live there

Before our residence permits were issued
we signed an outrageous contract
We were to obey the orders of the troop
and the cultivation process was top secret
And if we died from a landmine accident
we had to accept it—
our bodies were our collateral, so to speak

Also, there was a condition that
for one year, only men would move in temporarily

to cultivate minefields
under the military troop's command

대마리7
— 가 입주

전략촌에는
전 가족이 입주를 해서
오손도손 알콩달콩 살 수 없었다

우선 지뢰밭을 개간해서
농토를 마련하는 것이 급해서
남자들만 먼저 가 입주를 했다

전략촌으로 가는 날
다시 만날 기약 없는 가족들과
아침을 먹는 둥 마는 둥
남자들은 연장을 챙겨 들고
대마리로 갈 채비를 했다

먹을 식량과
간장 된장을 챙겨 넣고
읍사무소에 모여서
대마리 전략촌으로 이동을 했다

5검문소를 통과해서

장군들도 별판을 가리고 가야 하는
먼지 풀풀 날리는 신작로를 지날 때
쟁쟁하게 들리던 대남 방송은
마치 환영을 하는 소리 같았다.

Daemari 7

Temporary Residence

In the Strategy Town
the entire family could not
happily live together

It was urgent to clear the minefields
and open up new farmland
therefore males moved into the town first

On the day to the Strategy Town
Men took their tools and
got ready to go to Daemari
barely having breakfast
with families who it might be the last time to see

They packed food
including ganjang and doenjang
gathered at the town hall
then moved to Daemari Strategy Town

After passing through checkpoint 5
and passing a newly constructed dust-blowing

road
  where even generals had to hide rank-showing
stars on their cars
  vivid propaganda broadcasts from the North
  sounded like welcoming them

대마리8
—통제부 골짜기

사단장도 북한군 저격 때문에
별판을 가리고 다니는 길을 따라
가슴 쿵쿵쿵 졸이며
백오십여 명이 도착한 곳은
지금의 태양 초소 부근

북한 쪽에서 잘 보여
자랑하기 좋고
군인들이 통제하기 쉽게끔
야트막한 산들 사이에
시냇물이 흘러 물 걱정이 없는
통제부 골짜기

버드나무가 숲을 이룬 골짜기에는
북한군을 감시하는 망루가 서 있고
군부대 지휘소 검은 천막
민간인들이 살아야 할
네 개의 임시 천막 기다리고 있었다

우선, 독자 행동은 금물
굴비처럼 열 명씩 다니기 위해
아는 사람들끼리 조를 짰고
단 일주일 치 식량이
선물처럼 배급됐다.

Daemari 8

The Tongjebu Valley

Along the path where even the division commander
hides the stars on his car from the Northern snipers
with pounding heart
arrived a hundred and fifty
to near now called Taeyang-checkpoint

Easily observed from the North
therefore easy to boast
easy for soldiers to control
between low mountains
where the flowing stream provides enough water
is the Tongjebu Valley

In the valley where willows formed a forest
stood the watchtower monitoring the North Korean army
waited the black command post tent
and four temporary tents
where the civilians would live

First, individual actions were restricted
Familiar faces formed groups of ten
just like dried gulbi fish
No more than a week's provision
was allocated like a present to them

대마리9
— 군사훈련

어수선하게 전략촌에서
하루를 보내고
잠을 자려고 보니
텐트 안은 흙바닥 맨바닥이라
뼛속을 파고드는 냉기를 막으려고
버드나무를 잘라서 얼기설기
펼쳐 놓고 그 위에서
새우잠을 청했다

눈만 감으면
앞으로 일어날 일이 걱정이라
싱숭생숭 잠이 올 리가 없고
바로 옆에서 떠드는 잡소리 같이
귀를 후벼 파는 대남 방송 소리에
자는 둥 마는 둥 첫날밤을 보냈다

깜빡 잠이 든 것 같은데
기상나팔 소리에 겨우 일어나
아침은 먹었는지 기억도 안 나고

신병처럼 정신 교육을 받은 뒤에
일하다가 삽을 던져 버리고
총을 잡아야 하는 전투 대비 훈련

살아남기 위한 지형 숙달 연습을
사흘 동안 아주 지겹게 받았다

Daemari 9

Military Training

Spent a day
in the chaotic Strategic Village
Tried to sleep in a tent
on the bare floor covered with mud
Tried to sleep curled up
on the entangled pieces of willow
to prevent the bone-chilling cold

Close one's eyes
mind wanders without sleep
worrying the days to come
due to the babble noises of
earsplitting propaganda broadcast from the north
Spent the first night hardly sleeping

Dozed off with a flash
and barely woken up by the morning bugle
Can't even remember if I had breakfast
and received mental education like a recruit
Then, we dumped the shovel promptly at the time of duty

and grasped the gun in preparation for a battle

Trained to master the geographic features for survival
jadedly for three days

대마리10
— 산신제

비나이다 비나이다
한국 전쟁으로 만신창이가 된
통제부 골짜기 산신령님께
간절하게 빌고 또 비나이다

질긴 생명줄 끌고
오르지 살기 위해
대마리 전략촌까지 떠밀려 온
사람들이 두 손 모아 비나이다

혹시, 지뢰를 밟아도
뇌관이 고장 나서 터지지 않게 해주시고
자꾸만 집으로 돌아가고 싶어지는
갈대 같은 마음이 흔들리지 않게
꼭꼭 잡아 주시고

아비를 전략촌으로 보내고
북쪽에서 들리는 총소리에
심장이 덜컥 내려앉는

우리 가족들과
알콩달콩 살 수 있도록
넉넉한 아량을 베풀어 주소서

평생 神을 찾지 않던 사람들도
오늘 만큼은 공손히 머리를 조아리고
산신제 막걸리 잔을 올렸다

Daemari 10

Ritual for the Guardian Spirits

I pray I pray
I desperately pray
to our guardian spirits of the Tongjebu Valley
shattered by the Korean War

All the people who have dragged their lifelines
only with the wish to survive
to the Daemari village
pray with both hands

If, by any chance, we step on mines
please make sure that the detonator is broken
please help our fickle mentality
to hold the urge
to return home

Please share your generosity
until the day
our family can live happily ever after
although day by day our heart drops
with each gunshot from the North

after sending our father to the warzone

Even those who never sought after gods
bowed their heads down
and devoted a bowl of Makgeolli to the guardian spirits

대마리11

— 착공식

"준비!"

"폭파!"

이 소리가 들리자마자
태양교 건너편에서는
연기가 치솟아 오르고
대마리 벌판을 흔드는
폭음이 울려 퍼졌다

그 모습에 착공식을 찾아온
연천, 철원 군수와 읍면장
별을 단 장군들과 병사들
그리고 개척 단원들이
손바닥이 깨져라 박수를 쳤다

입으로는 함성을 지르며
즐거운 표정이었지만
마음속에서 고개를 쳐드는 두려움

갈대밭 어딘가에서
총을 든 북한 병사들이 우리를
노려보고 있을 것 같고

다 낡은 신발 밑에
뭉툭한 느낌이 올 때마다
지뢰 뇌관을 밟은 것 같아
식은땀이 흐르는
죽음보다 깊었던 절망

그걸 알지 못하는 귀빈들은
서둘러 착공 식장을 떠날 뿐이었다

Daemari 11

Groundbreaking Ceremony

"Ready!"
"Explode!"

Soon after hearing the sound
across Taeyanggyo
smoke soared and
the explosion sound
shaking Daemari field resonated

The scene gathered people at the groundbreaking ceremony
governors of Yeoncheon and Cheorwon
headmen of town
generals with rank-showing stars
soldiers
and pioneer group members
clapped so hard that their palms were about to break

Despite cheering shout
despite pleasant look

from deep in the heart, fear lifted its head

Somewhere in the reeds
it feels like armed North Korean soldiers
would stare hard at us

Under worn-out footwears
whenever something stumpy was sensed
it felt like stepping on a detonator of mine
Arousing despair deeper than death
making cold sweat run down

Honored guests who didn't know it
just left the site in a hurry

대마리12

— 막걸리 파티

막걸리를 마신다
근심을 담아 술잔을 부딪친다
착공식 손님들이 가져온
돼지고기 이백 근을 안주 삼아
막걸리 스무 말을 다 마신다

술을 못 마시는 사람도
술고래도 오늘은
허리끈을 풀어 놓고

내일부터 시작되는 개간에
지뢰를 밟아 두 다리가 잘려 나가고
숨통이 끊어질 것 같은
살 떨리는 공포를 잊기 위해
유행가에 젓가락 장단을 맞춰가며
마시고 또 마신다

밤을 새워 마시다가
소변을 핑계 삼아

텐트 밖을 나서
남쪽 하늘을 보면
걱정으로 지샐 여편네와
철모르는 자식들 초롱초롱한 눈망울이
아픈 별처럼 내려와
눈시울을 젖게 한다

Daemari 12

Makgeolli Party

We drink makgeolli
Raise our glasses with our worries
Snack on the 200-geun of pork
Brought by the ceremony's guests
and drink a drum of makgeolli

Those who cannot drink
Heavy drinkers too
All loosen their belts today

With the cultivation starting tomorrow
To forget the chilling horrors of
stepping on a mine and losing both legs
and getting quietus
We match the sound of our chopsticks
to the rhythm of popular songs
and drink and drink

While drinking through the night
I use the bathroom as an excuse
And go outside the tent

To look at the Southern sky
My wife staying up with worry
And the bright eyes of naive children
Come down like painful stars
And make my eyes water

대마리13
— 개척 시작 아침

지난밤에는
도저히 잠을 잘 수가 없었다

몸을 가눌 수 없도록
막걸리를 마시고
버드나무를 찍어서 깔아 놓은
침상에 누워 눈을 감아도
귓속말처럼 들리던 대남 방송 소리

갈대가 몸을 비비는 소리가
마치 누군가 다가오는 발자국 같아
화들짝 눈을 뜨면
가설 텐트 밖을 살금살금 맴도는
바람 소리에 잠을 잘 수가 없었다.

설핏 잠든 것 같은데
기상나팔 소리에 비몽사몽
서둘러 옷을 입고
통제부 골짜기를 흐르는

냇가에 나가서 목을 축이고

얼기설기 화덕을 걸고
보리가 섞인 쌀을 씻어
아침밥을 안치고
고추장, 된장을 풀어 넣은 반합을 걸고
네 맛인지 내 맛인지 모르는
찌개를 만들었다

Daemari 13

The Morning of the First Shovel

I couldn't sleep last night

I couldn't bear my own body
because of having drunk Makgeolli
Laying on a bed made of willow tree
I couldn't avoid the propaganda broadcasting from the North
which was like a whisper, with my eyes closed

Sounds of reed rubbing themselves
were like someone's upcoming footstep
I immediately woke up
and couldn't sleep again
because of a wind slickly roaming around a temporary tent

Maybe I slept a bit
With a wake-up horn, being half awake
I put my clothes on in a hurry and
drank some water of the Tongjebu Valley

Roughly putting a pot on a fireplace
washed a rice with some barley
and boiled the rice for a breakfast meal
Also made a stew
with doenjang and gochujang on a mess tin
hard to know what taste it was

대마리14
— 불 놓기 작업

개간 방법은 아주 간단했다

버드나무, 억새 우거진 들판에
불을 놓아서 다 태워 버리는 것이었다
그런 뒤에 지뢰를 캐내는
아주 간단한 방식이었다

부대장 일장 연설이 끝나고
군데군데 불을 놓자
살랑살랑 봄바람을 타고
슬금슬금 낮은 포복으로
퍼져 나가는 시뻘건 들불

사방팔방 불이 번지자
퍽~ 터지는 발목 지뢰
꽝~ 폭발하는 대전차 지뢰
정신없이 떼 지어 나오는 멧돼지 가족
겅중겅중 뛰어나오는 고라니 가족

이것보다 인민군이라도
엉금엉금 기어 나온다면
두둑한 포상금에 팔자 고친다는 생각에
침을 꼴깍 삼키며
매운 눈물로 바라보는
대마리 벌판에 들불

Daemari 14

Field Burning

Land clearing process was very simple:

make a fire and burn the fields
dense with willows and silvergrass
Then root out the mines
It was as simple as that

After the commander's speech
we made a fire here and there
Wafted by gentle spring breeze
the fire crept up on the field
spreading in crimson red

The fire was all over the place
BANG, when a toe popper blowed up
BOOM, and an anti-tank mine exploded
A boar family frantically fled in flocks
A water deer family joined in loping flight

But more importantly if
a single North Korean soldier crawled out

handsome bounty would turn our fortunes around
We smacked our lips cherishing the thought
while our eyes burned and watered
watching the wildfire on Daemari field

대마리15
— 민간인 지뢰 탐지기

개척에 앞장을 선 것은
지뢰를 탐지하는
민간인들이었다

값비싼 미제 라디오를 뜯어
부속품으로 본체를 꾸며
나무통에 넣어서 만든
허름한 지뢰 탐지기

선 하나는 리시버를 연결해서 귀에 꽂고
다른 선은 엉성한 매미채처럼 생긴 것에
끊어지지 않게 이어 놓은 뒤에

땅에다 이리저리 흔들다 보면
바늘 끝처럼 귀를 찌르는 진동으로
귀신같이 지뢰를 찾아내는
세상에서 가장 간단한 탐지기
그 시대에 최첨단 지뢰 탐지기

이것을 그럴듯하게 허리에 찬
비무장 민간인들이
사람들 발목을 기다리고 있는
대인 지뢰밭 속으로
당당하게 걸어 들어갔다

Daemari 15

The Civilian Mine Detectors

The firstcomers
were the mine-detecting
civilians

Very expensive American radio
ripped apart and put together
in a wooden box
became a humble mine detector

One line connected to a receiver
and plugged into an ear
One line connected to some crude dragonfly net

Hovering back and forth over the ground
finding mines like magic:
the simplest mine-detector in the world
the most advanced detector of the time

Unarmed civilians
wearing the gizmo like a prize
strode into the field

full of mines awaiting
for human ankles to come

대마리16
— 지뢰를 캐는 방법

지뢰를 캐는 데는
달랑 삽 한 자루만 있으면 OK
이유는 간단했다

사람 발목을 노리는 지뢰는
뿔처럼 나온 인계 철선
세 가닥을 땅 위로 나오게 했다

그래야 사람이 밟고
발목이 뎅강 날아갈 수 있어서
언제나 정성껏 똑바로 심었다

지뢰가 있다고 신호가 오면
삽을 비스듬히 찔러 넣을 때
소름이 살짝 돋기는 해도
딱딱한 느낌이 덜컥 닿으면
그 주위를 슬금슬금 파내면 된다

그렇게 캐내는 지뢰는

감자 이삭줍기 같기도 했는데
묻은 지가 얼마 안 되어
페인트 냄새가 나기도 했다

Daemari 16

How to Dig Out a Landmine

To dig out a landmine
you were OK with just a spade
and the reason was quite simple

Out for the ankles, the mines
had tripwires as horns
with three strands left out to sprout

so that when stepped on
the ankles can be hacked off
hence are always planted upright with care

When the signal triggers, a mine!
Though hairs prickle up the spine
slip the tilted spade in by the side
Against a thump, hard
carefully dig, dig around the mine

Digging out mines as such
was like gleaning for grain

not been buried for long
it also smelt of paint.

대마리17
— 대인지뢰 옮기기

캐 놓은 지뢰를 옮기는 것은
대마리 가입 주민 일이었다
처음 본 지뢰는 분유 깡통에
굵은 철사 세 개가
삐죽삐죽 나와 있었는데
이것을 밟으면 뻥하고
다리가 끊어진다고 했다

처음 지뢰를 만졌을 때
등골까지 서늘한 느낌
지뢰를 들고 모아두는
구덩이까지 가는 길은
행여 미끄러져서 사고가 날까
두 손으로 공손히 들고
조심조심 들어다 살며시 놓았다

그렇게 몇 번 옮기다 보니
인계 철선을 만지는 것으로는
터지지 않고 사람이 밟아야 폭발함을

어느새 알아 버리고
한 손에 서너 개씩 들고
툭툭 던져도 아무 이상이 없었다

그러다 보니
이게 진짜 터지는 물건인지
의심이 스멀스멀 들기 시작했다

Daemari 17

Moving Anti-personnel Mine

T'was the Daemari people's role
to move the dug up landmine
The first landmine I saw
had three thick wires
sticking out from a milk powder tin can
I was told that stepping on this would
rip off my leg

The chills running down my spine
when I first touched the mine
On the way to the pit
where we kept the demined
I held it like a relic
and placed it down with greatest care

Several times later
I learned that
Unless you step on it
touching the tripwire won't trigger the mine
Then I carried them
three or four in each hand

tossing them into the pit
caused no problem

There a question slipped to my mind
Does this thing even explode or not?

대마리18
— 지뢰 처리 방법

요즘에는 지뢰 하나 발견되면
세상이 떠들썩하고
언론들이 물고 뜯고 하지만
당시 처리 방법은
가장 단순했다

구덩이를 파 놓고
개척민들이 양손에 지뢰를
들고 와서 휙휙 던져 놓으면

공병대 군인들이
폭약을 하나 밀어 넣고
줄을 길게 길게 연결해
스위치는 누르면
지뢰들을 한꺼번에 다 터지고
엄청난 작업이 끝이 난다

근래 유행하는 불꽃놀이만 못해도
소리 하나는 천지를 흔들었다

우리들은 귀를 막고
버드나무 그루터기에 숨어서
담배 한 개비
물고 있으면 되었지만

화지리 쯤에서 살고 있던
우리 가족들이
대마리 쪽에서 나는 폭음에
안절부절못했다는 소리는
나중에 들었다.

Daemari 18

Mine Disposal Method

Nowadays, if a mine has been found
it would make the world bustle
the press tear them down in pieces, but
the processing method those days
were truly simple.

The settler handled landmines in both hands
and swiftly threw them
in a hole they digged

Combat engineers
shoved in explosives one by one
and connected the lengthy ropes
As the switch was pressed
the mines exploded all at once
and that enormous task finishes

Didn't seem as good as the trending fireworks
but the sound shook heaven and earth

We were fine

with one cigarette in our mouth
our hands cupped over our ears
and we dodged behind the willow or the stump

But I later heard that
our family
who lived around Hwajiri
were all jittered by the
explosive sound from Daemari

대마리19

— 털레기 국수

아슬아슬한 일을 마치고
긴 그림자를 끌고
비척비척 텐트로 돌아 온
남자들끼리 저녁을 해먹는다

집에서 가져 온 반찬
마누라가 준비한 부식
그리고 쌀과 보리가 있지만
너무 늦어서 제대로 해 먹기는 틀렸고
지뢰에 조마조마했던 찬 가슴을
뜨거운 것으로 달래고 싶어서
털레기 국수를 끓인다

때에 쩌든 검은 솥을 걸고
시금털털한 김치도 넣고
푸석 말라비틀어진 시래기도 넣고
먹다 남은 멸치 대가리도 넣고
감자, 된장, 고추장, 썩을 놈의 세상도
다 풀어 넣고 펄펄 끓이다가

마지막에 국수, 칼국수
가리지 않고 서리서리 집어 넣는다

그러면 가진 것 모두
탈탈 털어 넣었다고
그럴싸하게 별호가 붙여진 털레기 국수 완성
그릇이라고는 반합 뚜껑
젓가락 없는 사람은 버드나무 가지 꺾어
우르르 몰려들어서
정신없이 퍼먹다 보면
뱃속이 뜨뜻해지는
대마리표 털레기 국수

Daemari 19

All-in Noodle, Teollegi

Finished a life-threatening work
pulling a long shadow over a tent
with no strength to endure
enjoyed the dinner together, without wives

Although there were appetizers from home
side dishes prepared by wives
rice, and barley
it was too late to have fine supper
Instead, we made Teollegi noodles
to ease the mine-frightened cold heart
by having a hot meal

Hung a black, old stained-pot over a fire
Put a bitter-sour kimchi
Put a dry, crooked siraegi
Put a left-over anchovy's head
Put a potato, doenjang, gochujang, and the fucking world
into the pot and stir, and let them boil hard
At last, we put this and that noodle and udon

randomly

Then, all we had being put in a pot
the reason why being called Teollegi
only dish we had was mess tin
Someone who didn't have chopsticks
used willow tree branches
All together, devoured the noodle
warmed our tummy
it's the Daemari Teollegi noodle

대마리20

— 우리들의 항고(飯盒)

대마리 텐트촌에서는
그릇이 필요 없었다
일본 놈들이 버리고 간 항고가
냄비, 뚝배기, 대접, 그릇을 대신했다

항고가 뭐냐하면
일제시대 일본군들이
미국에게 맞장 뜨겠다고
철모르고 덤벼들 때
배낭에 매달고 다니던
시커먼 만능 식기 쯤 되는데

이것이 어찌어찌 굴러다니다가
대마리 개척민들의
애장품이 되었다

아침밥을 항고에 해서
뚜껑에 덜어서 곰곰한 김치를
쭉쭉 찢어 먹은 뒤에 다시

밥에다 김치와 고추장을 넣고
지뢰 캐러 나가서 점심때가 되면
작대기에 손잡이를 쭉 걸어서
불을 피우면 뜨끈뜨끈한 도시락이 되는

일을 마치고
흔들흔들 돌아올 때
안에 숟가락이 딸그락딸그락
대마리 빈 들판을 울리던 항고

Daemari 20

Our Hang-go

We needed no bowls
in Daemari tent village
We used Hang-go, dumped by Japs
instead of pans, pots, dishes and plates

Hang-go, which is
like an all-in-one bowl in dark charcoal color
that Japanese soldiers carried
tied to their backpack
when they recklessly provoked war
with the US

In the morning
rice was cooked in Hang-go
and ate with kimchi torn apart with hands
using the lid as a plate
After that,
kimchi and gochujang
were added to the rice
and we went out with it to clear the mines
When it's time for lunch

we hung its handle on a stick
and made a fire to make it a perfect warm meal

Finishing up the day,
when we trudged back to the village
with clattering spoon inside
Hang-go echoed the empty field of Daemari

대마리21

— 공병대 도자

새벽부터 낮은 중저음의 엔진 소리가
통제부 골짜기를 흔든다
잠이 덜 깬 사람들은
난리통에 불사조 같던
인민군 탱크가 떠올라
놀란 가슴으로 밖으로 뛰어 나왔다

희미한 안개 속에서
불쑥 나타난 것은
검은색의 공병대 불도저

이 중장비로
지뢰를 제거한 구역
버드나무들을 단박에 밀어 내고
곰보돌들도 다 빼내 버리고
평평하게 작업을 했다

만약, 미처 캐내지 못한
대전차 지뢰가 있다면

단박에 불도저의 캐터필러가 엿처럼 끊어지고
운전병은 온몸이 산산조각 나는
아찔하고 진땀나는 목숨 줄 걸린 작업

그런데 다행이도
그런 사고가 나지 않은 것은
대마리 기적이었다.

Daemari 21

The 'Dozer

Engine noises at dawn
shook the valley whole
Drowsy people
work up and ran out in panic
recalled the tanks during war
which were like phoenixes

But what appeared amidst the fog:
straight from the military,
a black bulldozer

With this heavy equipment
Uprooted the willows
weeded the pebbles
patted the earth
of the area where mines were removed

Consider an anti-tank mine
that we may have missed:
the dozer's chains would've broken like candy
the driver's bones would've split like lightning

It was quite miraculous a fact that
such a tragedy did not happen that day
in Daemari

대마리22

— 열 명씩 행동하기

텐트촌에서는 반드시
열 명씩 조를 짜서 행동을 했다

바로 눈앞에 보이는
북한군들이 어떤 짓을 할지 모르고
지뢰밭에서 일을 하다가
변을 당하더라도
신속하게 처리할 수 있어서
초등학생들처럼 열 명씩 무리지어
우르르 몰려다녔다

개간을 하러 나갈 때도
열 명씩 묶은 조별로 행동을 해야 해서
한 사람이 변소라도 가면
일을 볼 때 까지 아홉 명이
투덜거리며 기다려야 했다.

처음에는 쑥스럽고 불편도 했지만
시간이 지나면서 오랜 친구 같았고

전생에는 한 가족이었겠다는
생각을 많이도 했다

그러나 사실대로 말을 하자면
이름도 모르는 낯선 곳에서
혼자 죽을 수 있다는 것이 억울하고
같이 갈 친구들이 있다는 것이
가족보다 더 의지가 되었다

Daemari 22

Act by Ten

The tent-town always
had to act by ten

Because one can never know
What the soldiers from the North may do
Because even if while at a minefield
something happens
we can always be quick
We act by ten
like schoolchildren running around

Even when we cultivate land
we must always act by ten, by groups
Even if one goes to the outhouse
the other nine must wait
of course with some complaining and grumbling

At first it's embarrassing and uneasy
but as time goes by, we become like old friends
Sometimes we think
In our past lives, we might have been one family

But to speak frankly
dying alone here at a nameless place
feels unfair and wrong
And we rely on our companions who must leave, like I
more than even our own true family

대마리23
— 국민학교 터

열 명씩 떼를 지어서
가장 먼저 작업을 한 곳은
먹고 사는 논이 아니고
편안한 집터도 아니고
우리 자식들이 공부할 수 있는
국민학교 터를 닦는 것이었다

우리들이 목숨을 내놓고
지뢰 미확인 지대에 뛰어 든 것도
내 자식들에게는 지긋지긋한
가난을 물려주기 싫어서이고
뼛골 빠지는 농투성이보다는
편안히 책상머리에 앉아
펜대 굴리는 사람 만들고 싶어서였다

아무리 땅을 많이 준다고 해도
자식들이 마음 놓고 배울
우리 학교가 없다면
헛짓거리라는 생각

모처럼 애비 노릇을 하는 것 같아
삽자루를 단단히 움켜쥐고
콧노래를 부르며 찾아간 곳은

사시사철 햇살이 잘 들고
운동장으로 쓰기에 딱 맞는
넓은 들판이 기다리고 있는
지금의 백마고지역 근처였다

Daemari 23

The School Ground

The place the ten worked
first and foremost
wasn't a rice paddy for no starvation,
wasn't a ground for a cozy house,
but was a ground for a elementary school
where our children could learn

The reason we had came to this ground
where landmines lie anywhere
was because we did loathed
bequeathing poverty to our children
Instead of bone-breaking farmwork
we longed to make them adults who use pen
who sit down on a desk, and work with no worries

The thought that no matter how much land we leave behind
with no school
to study freely
it's all just crap

Maybe for the first time, I am acting as a father
I grasped the shovel handle tightly
humming a song, I walked along

To come to the ground where the sun shines all four seasons
where there could be the perfect playground
The huge field awaited
Only to become today's Baengmagoji station

대마리24
— 첫 지뢰 사고

생각만 해도 끔찍한
첫 지뢰 사고는
초등학교 터 작업에서 일어났다

지뢰를 캐낸 곳은
빨간 줄로 표시를 해 놓아
안전한 지역이었는데
사고가 나려고 그랬는지

탐지 작업도 하지 않은 곳에
쳐 놓인 줄을 보고
마음 놓고 갔다가
아뿔싸, 지뢰가 터졌다

꽝하는 소리도 잠시
검은 연기가 온몸을 휘감고
풀썩 쓰러진 사람 얼굴은
검은 흑빛 피투성이었다

살점이 너덜너덜하고
피가 철철 흐르는 다리를
허리끈을 풀어 조여 매고
군부대 지프차에 실려 가면서
사람들을 바라보던 간절한 눈빛

그날은 작업을 멈추고
텐트로 돌아와
아무 말도 못하고 술을 마셨다
안주도 변변치 않아
눈물을 찍어서 쓴 술을 마셨다

Daemari 24

The First Accident

The first landmine accident
that was so terrible at the bare thought
happened at the work of elementary school

The place where we dug mines
was marked with a red line
so it could be a safe area
but as if it was meant for an accident

Looking the line
at the place where there's no detection
relax without worrying and go there
Damn, a mine explode

The booming of landmine was a moment
black smoke whipped around the body
and the face of fallen man
was covered with black blood

The flesh was in tatters
His legs with flowing blood

was fastened with waist strap
and he was carried on military troop jeeps
with dying look watching people

We stopped the work that day
and came back to tent
just drank without saying a word
Because munchies are coarse
we dipped them into tears and drank

대마리25

— 개간을 포기하고 떠난 사람

“여보게 지금 떠나면 어떻게 하나”
“시작을 한 것 끝을 봐야지”

“아니요 여긴 사람 살 곳이 아니예요”
“어떤 미친놈이 돌보다
지뢰가 많은 땅을 개간을 한대요”
“차라리 죽으면 그만이지만
다리 병신이라도 되면
우리 가족은 어떻게 한대요“

첫 지뢰 사고가 난 밤
한숨을 푹푹 내쉬던
여주에서 온 두 형제가 보따리를 쌌다

땅 한 뙈기 없어서
평생 소작쟁이로 남을 것 같아
어떻게 해서든 논마지기를 마련해서
사람답게 살아 보겠다고
경기도 여주에서 물어물어 찾아온

두 형제가 다정하게 보따리를 싸서
뒤도 돌아보지 않고 귀향을 했다

먼지 풀풀 나는 길을 따라서
처량하게 떠나는 두 형제를
슬픈 눈으로 바라보던 사람들은
내일 다시 개간을 하기 위해
핏자국이 남아 있는 삽을 닦는다.

Daemari 25

The Man Who Abandoned Cultivation

"Look, how dare you leave now?"
"You ought to seize this chance as you started"

"No, I cannot stay here no more"
"What crazy man dare clear this land
with more mines than rocks"
"Being dead is better,
or worse what if I become disabled,
what will happen to my family then."

The night when the first accident happened
two brothers from Yeoju
sighed deeply with moons high
packed their bags for home

With no patch of field at their hands
With their worries of being lifelong tenant
With their dreams of having decent lives
To get just a piece of land
two brothers from Yeoju, Gyeonggi
hastefully packed their bags

together left the town without a backward glance

Following the roads with a cloud of dust
brothers leave the town ploddingly
Staring them with confusing eyes
people started to overhaul their spade bloodstain
still remains on
to cultivate the land, their land

대마리26

— 지뢰 사고 보상금 0원

돌멩이보다
지뢰가 더 많은 땅에서
일상적으로 일어나는
사고는 누구 책임일까

요즘 같으면 인권 단체들이 나서서
목소리 높여 거들어 주겠지만
당시에는 이유는 딱 한 가지였다
정말로 재수가 없어서
지지리 복이 없어서
일어난 개인적 책임이었다

발목이 끊어진 사고 치료비
개인이 알아서 부담
더 이상 일을 못하는 손해
지뢰는 밟은 개인 책임
후유증 보상이고 위자료는
애초 들어 본적도 없는 땅

이런 사고가 발생해도
어디에 하소연도 못했던 이유는
입주를 신청할 때
어떤 사고도 자부담이라는
지금의 신체 포기 각서보다 더 무서웠던
생명 포기 각서 때문이었다

이렇게 대마리에서는
대한민국은 없었고
스스로 알아서 지뢰밭을
개간을 해야 하는
불쌍한 개척민들만 있었다

Daemari 26

Compensation for Mine Accident: 0

On land with more mines
than stones
who is responsible
for daily accidents?

Today human rights groups would come forward
to speak up and help
but at the time there was only one reason
It was one's own burden
because one was unlucky
awfully unlucky

The cost of treating a broken ankle
was to be self-covered
the damage that made one unable to work
and stepping on mines were personal responsibilities
Compensation for aftereffects nor alimony were
unheard of in this land

Even if accidents like these happen

the reason for not complaining was
the paper we signed when moving in
for the abandonment of our lives
which demanded that we cover any accident by ourselves
even scarier than the abandonment of bodies

Like this, in Daemari
there was no Republic of Korea
but only the poor residents
who had to clear the minefields
on their own

대마리27

— 철책이 없었던 땅

그 당시에는 남북한의
경계가 없었다
멀리 보이는 북쪽 막사
우리 남쪽 막사 사이에는
철책조차 없었던 허허 벌판

북한군이 내려오면
단박에 잡아 버리겠다는 생각으로
철책을 칠 생각은 없었고
백마고지역 자리에 목책이 있었다

고물 캐러 오는 민간인을 통제하고
살금살금 내려온 공비들이 건드리면
딸랑딸랑 소리가 나도록
미제 통조림 깡통들이
주렁주렁 매달려 있었다

그래도 밤이면 북한군들이
살쾡이처럼 내려 와서

대광리에서 막걸리를 먹고 갔다
화지리에서는 쌀자루를 훔쳐 갔다
흉흉한 소문이 날마다 들렸다

그런 말을 들은 밤에는
몸은 피곤해도 잠은 오지 않고
텐트를 스쳐가는 바람 소리에
내게 배급된 칼빈 소총 자리를
눈으로 다시 한번 확인을 해야 했다

Daemari 27

A Land Without Iron Railings

At that time
there were no barriers
between the North and the South
Wild plain, not even iron railings
between the barracks of the South
and the North seen far away

With an idea of
overpowering North Korean army at once
were they to invade,
only a wooden fence stood at Baengmagoji station site

American tins hung in clusters
to control Civilians coming to collect junks
and to jingle at the touch of communist guerillas
stealthily invading the South

Still night after night
the North Korean soldiers would break in like wildcats

drank makgeolli in Daegwangri
and stole bags of rice from Hwajiri
Bleak rumors were to be heard every day

At nights when those rumors were told
hard to sleep despite the fatigue
And the sound of the wind passing through the tents
made me check again, with my own eyes
where my assigned Calvine rifle was

대마리28
— 해골 바가지

공병대 불도저가 밀어낸
나무뿌리를 파내다 보면
흔하게 나오는 것이
희멀건 뼈다귀들

애써 짐승 뼈들이라
생각을 하고 나무 등걸
모아 놓은 곳에 슬쩍 집어 던졌다

솔직하게 말을 하자면
처음 만졌을 때는
살이 떨리기도 했지만
너무 흔하게 나오다 보니
잘 마른 나무 토막처럼
아무 느낌도 나지 않았다

가끔, 허옇게 이빨을 드러내고
겸연쩍게 웃는 것 같은
해골바가지가 나오면

서둘러 땅에 묻어 버리고
아무렇지 않게 작업을 한 날 밤에는

해골바가지 귀신이
꿈속까지 찾아오기도 했었다

Daemari 28

Skull Ghost

Digging up the roots of the trees
which is shoved by a bulldozer
there are white bones
that can be seen commonly

Trying to think
they were animal bones
we just threw them away at a pile of woods

Honestly
at the first touch
they made shiver
But as they appeared so commonly
shiver disappeared
just like touching a piece of well-dried wood

Sometimes,
when awkwardly smiling
skull came out
we hurriedly buried it down
and started working

but at that night

a skull ghost appeared in a dream

대마리29
— 사망 사고

사람이 죽었다
지뢰를 밟았는데
운이 나쁘게도
한꺼번에 두 개가 터져서
대마리 곰보돌 밭에
검은 연기를 남기고
유언도 없이 사망을 했다

가마니로 시신을 수습해서
막사로 돌아왔지만
외지 사람이라
식구들이 올 때까지
텐트 밖에다 모셔 놓고
저녁 식사로
털레기 국수를 끓인다

처음에는 기가 막히고
겁도 나서 밥 생각이 없었는데
국수 가락 속에 김치 냄새에

습관적으로 젓가락을 들고
하나둘 모여든다

먹자고 하는 일
잘 먹고 살자고 하는 일
죽은 사람은 잊고
국수발을 씹는다

그렇게 먹다가
죽은 사람 빈자리가 생각나
아차하고 돌아보는
텐트 옆에 가마니 더미

거기서 털레기 국물 같은
핏물이 흐르고 있다.

Daemari 29

Fatal Accident

A man died
The man stepped on mines but
unfortunately,
two mines exploded at the same time
A man died
without a will,
only left black smoke
in Daemari variolitic yard

Retrieved the man's dead body
and brought it back to the barrack
But since the man was from the other region,
until his family arrived at the town,
we left him outside the tent
and for dinner,
boiled Teollegi noodles

At first, it was ridiculous and scary to eat something
But by force of habit,
people brought chopsticks to the smell of kimchi

from the noodles
  and came one by one

It's for eating well,
eating well and living better
Forget the dead
Just chew the noodles

Suddenly,
the dead man's empty space came to mind
so turned and looked back
the piles of rice bags next to the tent

There, the blood
looks like the soup of the Teollegi
was running out

대마리30
— 보리 두 말

금학산이 핏빛 노을을 펼쳐 놓고
똥개들이 악머구리처럼 울고 있는데
집 앞에 십자가 표시를 한
지프차가 저승사자처럼 찾아 왔다

어찌할거나 사태를 직감한
팔순 노모 손은 바람처럼 떨고
동생은 입술을 깨물고
지프차를 맞아 들였다

덜컥, 차 뒷문이 열리고
군용 모포로 감싼 시신을
병사들이 조심조심
안방에 내려놓는다

무언가 할 말이 있는데
목구멍으로 뜨거운 것이 치밀어
가슴을 팍팍 치고 싶은데
인솔 장교는 보리 두 말을

조의금인양 마루에 내려놓고
절 대신 거수경례를 올려붙이고는
쌩하니 돌아갔다

그래도 지뢰에 잘려나간
다리 없는 초상은 지낼 수 없어
아버지는 지푸라기로
가짜 다리를 만들어야 했다

Daemari 30

Two-mal of Barley

Blood-red sunset spilled over Geumhak Mountain
and village dogs howled like noisy frogs
when a jeep with a cross mark on it
arrived in front of the house

What's do be done? — Her hands shivering like the wind
the mother, now eighty, sensed right away something's wrong
and my sister, bit her lips
and let the jeep in

The back door of the car opens with a clack
and soldiers carefully
put the corpse wrapped in military blanket
down on the floor

There is something I have to say
something hot jolts up my throat
and I want to beat my chest
but the officer in charge laid two-mal of barley

on the floor, like some death money
saluted instead of bowing
and turned his back and peeled out

We still could not have a funeral
with his legs blown off by a mine
so my father
had to get fake legs made of hay

대마리31
— 지푸라기 다리

지뢰 사고로 다리 잘려 죽은 친구를
그냥 장사를 지낼 수는 없어
의족을 만들어 초상을 치렀다

하늘 나라에 가서도
다리 병신 취급 받을 것 같아
지푸라기로 만든 다리를
그럴싸하게 달아매었다

짚풀 다리는 만들기 쉬워도
살점이 꺼멓게 말라붙었고
핏줄이 끊어진 실처럼 보이고
사람 썩는 냄새로
고개가 절로 돌아가는
지푸라기 다리를 붙일 때
흐르는 땀 속에 섞였던 눈물을
누가 기억이나 할까

미처 감지 못한 두 눈빛이

무섭고 애처로워 다시 쓸어내려 주고
서둘러 나올 때
여보게 부르는 소리가 들리는 듯
자꾸만 돌아보게 되는
절망을 그 누가 알고 있을까

Daemari 31

Haystack Leg

We couldn't send
Away our dead friend, legless
so we made him an artificial one

We tied the leg together
so that he wouldn't be treated
as a freak
in heaven

It may be easy to make a leg out of haystack
but who would remember
the tears streaming down our face
as we attach the haystack
the stench from the blackened flesh hanging
the veins that look like torn strings
that instinctively makes heads turn the other way

But who would remember
The despair
as we closed shut those two pitiful eyes
as we hurried out

as if we would hear his calls
for help behind us

대마리32

— 비 내리는 날

아침을 대강대강 때우고
밀린 잠이나 청하려고
누워 있으려니
집에 있을 마누라가 그립고
자식들이 보고 싶어
잠이 안 온다

낡은 텐트를 흔드는 천둥이 치면
난리 통에 들었던 폿소리
머릿속에 지뢰들이
한꺼번에 터지는 것 같아
참다못한 사람들이
하나 둘 모여서
울컥울컥 치미는 슬픔을 달래려
막소주를 마신다

아침에 먹다 남은
김치 조각을 안주로
너도 한 잔 나도 한 잔

반합을 두드리는 젓가락 장단에 맞춰
오랜만에 노래를 부른다

알량한 김치 안주가 떨어지면
굵은 왕소금을 서너 알씩 먹으며
짜고 쓰기만 한 막소주를 마셨다

그런 날이면 대마리 벌판에서는
지뢰 사고로 이리저리 튀었던
핏자국 딱지들이
빗물에 말끔하게 지워지고 있었다

Daemari 32

A Rainy Day

Barely ate breakfast
trying to catch up on some sleep
I lied down on bed
Missing wife at home
longing for sons and daughters
I can barely fall asleep

When thunder shakes the old tent
all at once
landmine and boom of cannons explode in my mind
I can no longer bare it
One by one people gather around
and drink cheap soju
hoping
It would ease their surging sorrow

With some uneaten Kimchi from breakfast
we drink
You
and then me

to the rhythm of chopsticks striking rice bowl
we sing after a long time

When we run out of Kimchi
then with three or four grains of coarse salt
we drank
only to feel bitter and salty taste

At those days in Daemari field
scab and bloodstains
splattered here and there in landmine explosion
were being washed away
cleanly
in the rain

대마리33

— 비트

"비트를 발견하면 꼭 신고하세요."

작업 나가기 전에 대대장이
항상 입에 달고 하는 말

비트는 북한 간첩들이
연천 대광리 쪽이나
철원 화지리 방향으로
야금야금 이동하던 길에서
잠시 쉬기 위해 야트막한 능선에
구덩이를 파 놓은 은신처

철책도 없는 휴전선이라
북한 간첩들이
풀 방구리에 쥐 드나들 듯 해서
비트가 군데군데 많았다

그렇다고 순진하게 신고를 했다가는
온 부대에 비상이 걸려

하루 작업을 종치는 일이라
봐도 못 본 척 했었지만

가끔 비트 안에서
술에 골아 떨어진
정신 나간 간첩이 있으면
목을 비틀어다 신고한
두둑한 포상금으로
이 지긋지긋한
지뢰밭을 벗어나는 것은
숨겨진 우리들 꿈이기도 했다

Daemari 33

Biteu

"If you find a biteu, make sure to report it."

said the battalion commander
whenever he went to work

Biteu is a hiding place
where North Korean spies dug holes
in a low ridge to rest for a while
on the way to
Yeoncheon Daegwangri
or Cheorwon Hwajiri

There were many biteu
because North Korean spies
came and went incessantly
as the border has no barbed wire fence

But if we had naively reported the biteu
the whole unit would have put on alert
and that day's work would have been over
so we pretended we didn't see it

But it was also our hidden dream
to get out of
this gruesome minefield
with a hefty reward
for reporting
a drunken crazy spy
in the biteu

대마리34
— 일주일 만에 외출

통제부 골짜기는
유배지와 같았다

개간을 하러 나갈 때도
조기 한 두릅처럼 열 명씩 이동하고
텐트로 돌아와서는
개인적 외출이 허락되지 않는
반쯤은 군대 생활이었다

그러나 일주일 정도 지나면
가지고 온 부식들이
밑바닥을 보이고
가족에 대한 그리움이 치솟을 때
부식 조달 외출이 허락되었다

외출을 나가기 전날 밤에는
오랜만에 가족을 본다는 기쁨에
잠을 설치기도 했고
아침에는 밥을 먹는 둥 마는 둥

면도를 곱게 하고
집으로 향했다

지옥 같은 땅을 잠시라도
벗어난다는 생각에
신작로에서 풀풀 나는
흙먼지도 향기롭게 느껴졌다.

Daemari 34

Going Out in a Week

The valley was
no more than a place of exile

When we went out to cultivate
we moved in groups of ten, like a string of croak-
ers
After coming back to the tent
any private outings disallowed
It was halfway military life

After about a week
when the snakcs we brought
were all eaten up
And when the longing for our families soared
finally we were allowed to go out and bring some
snacks

The night before going home
we couldn't fall asleep
excited to meet our family
took the breakfast in a flurry

All perfectly shaved
we Headed home

Escaping the hellish place
just for a moment
made the smell of the dust
of a newly built road sweet

대마리35

— 경기도 여주 사람들의 주말

철원, 연천 사람들은
주말이면 부식을 가지러
집에 돌아 갈 수 있었지만
길이 멀어 어쩌지 못하고
통제부 텐트를 지켜야 했던
경기도 여주에서 온 사람들

어찌어찌 귀동냥으로 듣고
대마리로 개간을 한다고 나설 때
정말 지뢰가 깔린 죽음의 땅인지는
꿈속에서조차 상상하지 못했던 여주 사람들

첫 지뢰 사고가 터지자
몇몇 친구들이 돌아갈 때
마음속으로는 열 번도 넘게
짐을 쌌다 풀었지만

평생 소작인으로 남기 싫어
논 서른 마지기 주인 되는 것을

위안으로 잠든 밤에도
꿈속까지 따라 온 지뢰를 밟아
화들짝 깨서 식은땀을 닦았던 것보다도

주말이면 썰렁한 텐트에서
서넛이 모여 밥을 해 먹고
눅눅한 이불을 당겨
남몰래 눈물을 찍어내던
경기도 여주 사람들

Daemari 35

Weekends of People from Yeoju

Those from Cheorwon and Yeoncheon
could return home on weekends
to bring some food in
But the long road home
kept others, from Yeoju
in the tent inside the Tongjebu Valley

Heading for Daemari to reclaim field
after just hearing from someone
the people from Yeoju never expected
that minefields and deaths could await

When some quit
after the first mine accident
those who remained packed up countless times
inside their minds

Dreams of escaping a life of tenancy
and owning thirty-majigi to farm
became their lullaby
They wiped cold sweat off

when mines haunted them in dreams

Will anyone remember the sorrow of
the people from Yeoju
and their lonely weekends in the barren tents
having meals
and sheding tears
hiding behind a damp blanket?

대마리36
— 남편이 오는 주말

무소식이 희소식이던 남편이
부식을 가지러 오는 날
부인들에게는 설레임과
없는 살림에 걱정이 앞선다

낡은 자전거를 타고 온 남편
마당에 들어서자마자
군수품 조달 명령 하듯이

"된장, 김치, 국수 사리, 쌀 두어 되..."

된장은 담가 놓은 것이 있고
텃밭에 열무를 뽑아 절이고
국수는 사방 공사에서 받은 밀가루로
눌러 놓은 것이 있어 다행이고
이미 바닥난 쌀은
장리로 꾸어 올 궁리를 하는데

새끼들 한번 안아주지도 않고

친구들과 막걸리 마시러 나간 남편
통금 시간에 맞춰 들어와
정말 궁금한 대마리 사정은
들어 볼 기회도 없었다

다음 날에도
점심 때 한참 지나 일어나
말 한 마디 제대로 건네지 못하고
부랴부랴 부식을 자전거에 싣고
지뢰밭 뿐인 대마리로 향하던
남편을 뒷모습을 바라보며
부인네들이 간절하게 빌었던 소원 하나

"다음 주도 무사히 제발..."

Daemari 36

Husband Coming Weekend

After the days of no news being good news
when husband came home to get food
the wives were excited
but worry prevails over their poverty

Husband came on an old bicycle
and as soon as entering the yard
asked like ordering military supplies

"Doenjang, Kimchi, Noodles, Rice…"

Some Doenjang has been prepared beforehand
radishes have been pulled and pickled
luckily, noodles have been pressed
with flour received after the erosion control work
and rice that ran out already
was to be borrowed with interest

He went out for Makkoli with friends
without giving a single hug to the kids
Came in just in time for the curfew

so there was no chance to hear about
the situation of Daemari

Even on the next day
husband woke up long after lunch
so there was no time for a proper talk
Looking at his back
hurriedly loading food on the bike
and heading for Daemari only full of minefields
the wives prayed one wish

"Please be safe at least until the next weekend..."

대마리37
— 조명탄

개간 작업에 지쳐 잠을 자는데
갑자기 비상이 걸리고
태양 초소 부근이
대낮처럼 환하다

깊은 어둠을 타고
슬금슬금 내려오던
북한 간첩이 들켰는지
조명탄이 계속 날아다닌다

개미 새끼가 보일 정도로
환한 불빛 아래
군인들이 잔뜩 몰려가고
우리들도 칼빈 총을 들고
텐트 안에서 대기 중이다

금방 끝날 것 같던 작전이
밤새도록 지속된다
이러다 전쟁이 나는 것은 아닐까

이러다 우리도 전투를 해야 하는 것은 아닐까

싸늘한 총을 꼭 쥐고
불길한 생각도 잠시
피곤에 깜빡 잠이 들었다 깨도
아직도 비상 중이란다

조명탄 불빛을 보고
화지리 근처 집에서는
가족들도 걱정의 밤을 보낼 것이다

Daemari 37

The Flares

Exhausted by land clearing work, we slept
suddenly an emergency alert was put
and near Taeyang sentry post was
as bright as day

under the depths of night
stealthily coming down
North Korean spy perhaps was caught
flares fly over and over again

Under a bright light
where even a little ant can be seen
a number of soldiers flocked
we were also holding carbines
and on call in the tent

The operation that seemed to end soon
lasts all night
Maybe it'll lead to a war?
Maybe we are going to participate in a war?

With a cold gun
an ominous thought was a moment
fell asleep with being tired and even if I wake up
we are still in emergency

Watching the light of flares
in the house near Hwajiri
families will have an anxious night

대마리38
— 불침번

"어느 부대에서 불침번이 자는 바람에
간첩에게 일개 분대 병사들 목이 잘렸다."

근거도 없는 소문에
통제부 골짜기 텐트 사람들도
긴장을 하고 불침번을 섰다

민간인들에게까지
해코지를 하겠냐
생각을 하다가도
목이 없는 귀신이 되기는 싫어
졸린 눈을 비벼가며
불도 없는 텐트를 지키고 있었다

일에 지친 사람들의 잠꼬대
이를 가는 소리
이리저리 뒤척이는 기척
가끔 밖에서 들리는 군인들
근무 교대 소리에

깜빡 졸던 고개를 들었고

소변이라도 보려고
텐트 밖을 나서면
답답한 남쪽, 북쪽 하늘을
섬뜩하게 가르는 별똥 불빛 궤적
마치 내게 날아오는 대포 같아 화들짝 놀랐다.

Daemari 38

Night Watchman

"Some squad's sentry was asleep on watch
which let a spy from the North sneak in and slit their throats"

To such absurd rumors
even those in the Tongjebu Valley
stood watch in fear

Even while thinking:
There's no way
they would even harm civilians
Not wanting to become a headless ghost
rubbing tired eyes
we kept watch over a lightless tent

The sleeptalk of those tired from work
The sounds of grinding teeth
The tossing and turning, here and there
The sounds of the soldiers outside, changing shifts
would jolt our dozing selves awake

When, for a breath of fresh air
I took a step outside
The shooting stars which split the suffocating sky
cleanly into north and south
seemed to me like flying shells
and I jumped in fear

대마리39
— 측량기사

"여기, 지뢰 없어요"

토지 개량 조합에서 측량 나온
젊은이들 첫 마디였다

측량 장비를 내려놓고
시뻘겋게 뒤집힌 대마리 들판
군데군데 지뢰가 쌓인 구덩이를 보고
기겁을 하던 측량 기사들

그런데 기사들이야 측량기에 서서
계산을 하면 되지만
폴대를 들고 이리저리
왔다 갔다 하는 보조 기사들에게는
당장 지뢰가 터져
발목이 끊어질 것 같은 공포에
엉거주춤 꽁지 빠진
장끼들 같았다

첫날, 점심 때 보니
힘든 일도 하지 않았는데
작업복이 땀에 다 젖었고
밥을 먹는 손이
중풍 맞은 듯 와들와들 떨고 있었다

우리들은 짐짓 못 본 체 하면서
내가 가질 수 있는
서른 마지기가 어디쯤일까
즐거운 상상을 했다

Daemari 39

Surveyor

"There's no mine here"

were the first words from young men
from Land Improvement Association

After laying down the equipments
surveyors were appalled to see
mines piled up in pits
scattered on Daemari fields

While the senior surveyors could calculate
just standing beside the instrument
the assistant surveyors
pacing back and forth with poles
feared the mines would blow up any moment
and maim their ankles
So they walked awkwardly
like pheasants with their tails pulled off

On the first day, we saw them at lunch
Even though they didn't do any hard work

work clothes were soaked with sweat
and their hands
were shaking as if hit by a stroke

We pretended we didn't notice
and happily wondered
where our thirty-majigi would be
when we got to have the land

대마리40

— 대전차 지뢰 논둑

측량을 마치고
경계 말뚝을 치면
우리는 논둑을 만들었다

세 명이 한 조가 되어
가래질을 했다
내 논이 만들어진다는 생각에
팔이 아픈 줄도 모르고
콧노래를 부르며 가래질을 했다

그러나 맨땅으로 만든
논둑은 맥아리가 없이 자꾸만 무너져
곰보돌을 굴려다 넣으니
울퉁불퉁한 꼴에
맨발로 다닐 수 없을 정도로 엉망이었다

그런데 누가 어른 열 명이 올라가도
터지지 않는 대전차 지뢰
파란색 페인트 냄새가 풀풀 나는

둥그렇고 평편한 대전차 지뢰
올려놓으니 참으로 그럴싸했다

대전차 지뢰 한켜 놓고
흙으로 덥고
또 대전차 지뢰 한 켜 쌓고
흙을 정성스레 덮으니
보기도 좋고 무너지지 않는
든든한 논둑이 되었다

물론, 일을 마치고
대전차 지뢰 논둑을
밟으며 올 때는
섬뜩한 느낌이 났었다

Daemari 40

The Bank of Antitank Mine

After surveying
and staking out a boundary
we made the bank

Three persons as one team
we did spading
Feeling no pain
in sweet dreams of our own field being made
we did spading with humming

However the bank made of soil alone
was too weak and crumbled again and again
So we rolled perforated rocks in it but
the bank became raggedly ugly that
hard to walk barefooted

Then someone
used the antitank mines which
did not blow up even if ten grown man stand on
it

With the round and flat mines
smelling of blue paint were added
finally the bank looked truly better

One layer of antitank mines
covered with soil
and another layer of antitank mines
carefully covered with soil again
became a fine bank
nice and sound

Of course,
on the way back after work
walking on the bank of antitank mines
was quiet creepy

대마리41
— 양수기

"양수기를 설치하러 갈 사람"

통제소 단장의 소리에
지뢰밭이 무섭지 않던
호랑이 같은 사람들도
숨을 죽이고 꼴깍 침을 삼켰다

백마고지 전투 직전
중공군들이 봉래호를 폭파해
먼지 풀풀 나는 역곡천에
물줄기를 대는 양수기 작업

물이 필요한 것은
누구나 알고 있지만
북한 초소가 빤히 보이는
발동기를 놔야 하는데
목숨을 걸어야 하는 상황이라
누구 하나 선 듯 나설 수 없었다

군부대 무장 병력들이
좌우로 따라 붙어서
엄호를 한다고 해도
목숨을 내놓는 일이라

대인 지뢰 쯤이야
눈을 딱 감고 다리 하나만
내놓으면 되지만
총에 맞으면
목숨을 내놓은 일이라서

이 눈치 저 눈치 보면서
괜히 먼 산만 보고 있었다

Daemari 41

Water Pump

"Who wants to go to install the water pump?"

At the voice of the head of the control center
even those like tigers
who are not afraid of minefields
hold their breath and gulped

The water pump is for watering
the dusty Yeokgok-cheon
which were dried
because of Chinese communist army blew up Bongnae-ho
right before the Baengmagoji Battle

No one readily volunteer
Everyone knows
we needed water
but since we need to put the motor
where the North Korea's guard post could be seen so clearly
we had to risk our lives

Even if the arm forces in the military
tag along left and right
guarding us,
It risks our lives

If we step on anti-personnel mines,
we can just give up one of our leg
But if we get shot
we need to give up our lives

Therefore, walk on eggshells
and just look elsewhere

대마리42
— 양수기와 부비 트랩

노심초사했던 것과는 달리
무사히 양수기를 설치하고
바짝 바른 용강천에
물이 들어오기 시작했다

세상에서 가장 보기 좋을 일이
자식 입에 음식이 들어가는 것
논에 물이 들어가는 것이라

지뢰 캐는 일을 하다가도
개간한 땅의 흙을 적시며
반짝반짝 흐르는 것을 보면
이 고생이 끝나가는 것 같아
눈물이 나기도 했다

그런데 사흘 만에 양수기는
고장이 났는지 멈춰
다시 현장에 나가야했는데

누군가 기름이 들어가는
고무호스를 잘라버려
다시 연결을 하기 위해
여러 명이 양수기를 드는 순간

몰래 설치한 부비 트랩이
꽝~ 하고 한꺼번에 터져
사람들 손목이 다 날아갔다

그때 빤히 보이는
북한 초소에서는
환호성과 박수 소리가
환청처럼 들렸다

Daemari 42

Water Pump and Booby Trap

Unlike our worries
the pump was set successfully
and water began to fill
the dry brook

The most happiest thing to see is
food going into our child's mouth and
water going into our paddy

While digging the landmines
when we watched the glittery stream
watering the fresh land
tears suddenly flowed thinking
this pain would be end soon

But after only three days
water pump stopped, as if broken down
so we had to check the site

It turned out someone
cut the rubber hose where fuel flowed

At the moment we lifted the motor
to reconnect

A Secret booby trap
BOOM! blowed up at once and
all our hands were severed

That moment
shout and applause for joy
from the North Korean post
which could be seen so clearly
were heard like a ghost

대마리43
— 우렁이

하천에는 우렁이가
득시글거렸다

전쟁 가운데 있었던 땅이라
폭격에 맞아 죽거나
당시 지독하게 떠돌던
염병에 사람이 죽으면
땅에다 묻을 여유가 없어
그냥 하천에 던져 버렸다

물 위를 떠다니는 시체 위에는
금파리 떼들이 붙어 알을 낳고
구더기들이 득시글거렸고
물속에서는 우렁이들이
썩어 문드러진 살점을 뜯어 먹어서
하천마다 우렁이들이
바글바글했다

그 모습에 치를 떨던

어른들은 우렁이를
절대로 먹지 않았지만

먹을 것이 부실했던
대마리 개척민들은
일을 마치고 돌아오는 길에
살이 통통 오른 우렁이를 잡아다
끓여 먹었다

피 냄새 나는 것 같은
우렁이 질긴 살을
씹고 또 씹어 먹었다

Daemari 43

River Snails

The river was
swarming with snails

When people died from explosions
on the land amidst war
or died from the germs that
never quit roaming,
the remains were just tossed into the river
as it was too swamped for a burial

On the remains floating on water
a swarm of blowflies settled to lay their eggs
maggots clustered,
and underwater, the river snails
nibbled on the rotten flesh
Hence every river
overflowed with snails

The grownups who
winced from the sight
never dared eat the snails

but the Daemari settlers
who were faint from hunger
collected the plump river snails
on their way back from work
and boiled to eat them.

They chomped and chomped
the tough snail flesh
that seemed to smell like blood

대마리44
— 조카 면회

“사단장도 지프차에 별판을 가리고
들어오는 곳이라 안 돼요.”

“아니, 우리나라 육군 하사가
내 땅에 못 다닌다는 말이요.”

비가 부슬부슬 오는 날
난리 통에 부모를 잃어버려
업어 키운 조카가
계급장이 빛나는 육군 하사가 되어
대마리 텐트촌을 물어물어
검문소에 와 있다는 기별을 듣고
사정사정을 하는 김씨의 간청도

통제부 골짜기 텐트로
데리고 와서
단 몇 시간이라도
같이 있고 싶은 김씨의
간절한 소원도

단칼에 거절되었다

실랑이를 포기하고
낡은 자전거를 타고 나가
검문소 초소병 눈치 때문에
짧은 면회를 마치고
빗물 눈물범벅되어 돌아 설 때
조카는 슬픈 인사를 했다

"충성!"

Daemari 44

Visit

"You can't, this place is where
even a commander should hide his plate to come in"

"What? A sergeant in this country
can't even tread on his ground?"

On a softly rainy day
Had lost parents on that frantic day
Kim's nephew, like a son
became a sergeant, his proud son
Kim wander through Daemari village
to visit his nephew at the checkpoint
Though he begged to see him

Wanted to bring him to a tent
to the Valley near the base
For just a few hours
to be with his nephew
Though he begged to see him
his only wish got directly rejected

He gave up trying
Ride on his old bicycle just like
walking on a tightrope because of a guard
After the very short visit
his face smudged with tears and rains
His nephew said sad goodbye in rains

"Salute!"

대마리45

— 진달래 꽃 아래서

사방으로 불을 놓아
새까맣게 그을린 땅
개간 작업으로
시뻘겋게 뒤집힌 땅

세상의 시간이 멈춘 것 같은
이곳에도 봄이 찾아오고
산골짜기 능선을 따라
진달래꽃이 핀다

이름 모를 새들도
불에 그슬린 진달래 가지를 쥐고 앉아
악머구리 같은 대북 방송에
울음 자락을 섞고

진달래꽃 붉은 색에
빨갱이들이 떠올라
화들짝 놀라는 발아래
난리 통에 죽은 혼들이

몇이나 묻혀 있을까

이런 생각도 잠시
비상이 걸려 작업을 못하는 우리들은
통제부 진달래꽃 그늘 아래서
오랜 만에 지급 받은 칼빈 총을 닦는다

Daemari 45

Under an Azalea

A land burned black
by the fire laid on all quarters
A land flipped crimson
from the reclamation work

Spring somehow finds its way
to where the time of the world seems to have halt-
ed
and along the ridge of the glen
blooms an Azalea

Even the nameless birds
sit while clenching the Azalea stem withered from
flame
and cry to join the ribbiting propaganda
sent to the North

While we jump from the blush of the Azalea
that reminds us of the Reds
how many souls lost in turmoil
are buried beneath our alarmed feet?

So much for a moment of thought
Restrained from work due to an emergency alert
we stay in the control department, under the shade of Azalea
polishing the Carbine supplied for the first time in a while

대마리46
— 고라니 새끼

"도랑에 고라니 어미와 새끼가
잠을 자고 있더라니까"

"어미 목을 한 발로 밟고
다른 발로 새끼도 밟으려고 했는데
아, 그 놈이 글쎄, 잠든 새끼 배때지를
발로 차서 도망을 가서 못 잡았네, 그려"

고라니를 잡은 李氏
무용담을 떠벌리면서
축 늘어진 것을
작대기에 묶어서 가져왔다

전직 푸줏간 출신 김씨는
통제부 골짜기 냇가에서
고리니 털을 밀어냈고
작대기를 꿰뚫어 통째로 구웠다

오랜만에 고기 냄새를 맡은
개척민들은 너나 할 것 없이
아귀처럼 뜯어 먹었고
밤이 늦도록 술을 마셨다

새벽녘에 소변을 보던 김씨가
통제부 골짜기 끝자락에서
물을 따라 떠내려간
어미 털 냄새를 맡고 있던
새끼 고라니가 화들짝
도망가는 것을 봤다는
미안한 이야기를 했다

Daemari 46

Baby Water Deer

"A mother and a baby water deer were
sleeping in the ditch"

"I stepped on the mother's neck
and tried to step on the baby's too
Oh well, she kicked the sleeping baby's belly to wake
The baby ran, so I missed it"

Mr. Lee, who caught the water deer
Giving a rambling talk
brought the drooped body
tied up to a stick

Mr. Kim, who used to be a butcher
plucked it
at the streamside of The Tongjebu Valley and
skewered it, roasted it

Smelling roasted meat after a long time
everybody in the village

rushed to it like starving demons and
drank all night long

Mr.Kim, who went for a pee at dawn
told an uncomfortable story that
he saw the baby deer
smelling its mother's fur
drifting down the stream
at the edge of the Tongjebu Valley
jumped and run away

대마리47
— 현무암 위에 집터

"자네 들었나"

"집 지을 데가
곰보돌 너래바우가 깔린 곳이라네"

지긋지긋한 텐트촌 생활을 끝내고
가족들과 같이 살 집을
정부에서 지어 준다는 말에
기대에 찼던 사람들이

곰보돌이 많아서
개간조차 포기한
울퉁불퉁 돌밭이라는 소리에
귀를 의심했다

검은 암반을 깨는
터파기 공사를 하려면
곡괭이 가지고 할 수 없는 일

생고생을 해서 집을 짓는다 해도
바위에서 샘이 솟을 일은 없어
먹는 물은 어디서 구하고
배수로는 어떻게 내라는 말인지

사람들은 가슴에 바위를 얹은 듯
일은 손에 잡히지 않고
집터 측량을 하는 공무원들에게
눈치를 보며 하소연을 해도
계획은 바뀌지 않았다

이유는
단 한 가지
북한 땅에서 잘 보여
집 자랑하기에
딱 좋은 명당 터라는 것이었다.

Daemari 47

House on Basalt

"Did you hear the news?"

"The site for the house
Is full of perforated rock."

People full of excitement
For leaving the tent
For new houses built
By the government

Could hardly believe their ears
That the site was a field perforated rock
So harsh that it was even
Impossible to plow

One cannot break bedrock
And prepare the ground
With a single pickax

And if one was to build a house
No water ever springs from stone

Where was one meant to find a drink,
How was one meant to build a pipe?

Every heart held a boulder
No hand could hold an ax
Each tongue spoke of hardship
To officials surveying the land
But no plan ever changed

The single
Reason why:
The site was clearly seen from the north
And therefore perfect
To show off the houses

대마리48

— 붕어빵 같은 집짓기

집을 짓는 법은
아주 간단하고 단호했다

일렬 종대로 줄을 세운 듯
좌우로 정열해서 수평을 맞춘 듯
바둑판처럼 한 치의 오차도 없이
줄을 쳐 놓고 기초를 팠다

큰 바위가 나와도
줄을 벗어날 수 없어
손에 물집이 터지도록
곡괭이질을 해서 암반을 다 깨냈다

벽의 높이도 같아야 하고
지붕 처마가 약간만 벗어나도
당장 불호령이 떨어졌다

창문 위치도
지붕 색깔도 모두 같아서

마치 잘 정돈된 군대 막사 같았다

그렇게 지어야
북한 쪽이 부러워할 것이라는
근거 없는 믿음이 있었다

정작 문제는
더운 여름에 문을 열면
첫 집에서 부터 끝 집까지
시원하게 다 보인다는 것이었다

Daemari 48

Houses Like Bungeoppang

The recipe for housebuilding
Was simple and firm

Lined up single file
Balanced left and right
Lines were drawn and ground was built
Flawless as a checkerboard

People broke the bedrock
Till their hands were blistered
For no rock, large or small,
Was allowed to break the line

The walls must be of equal height
The eaves must look the same in sight
Or orders harsh would sound

Identical windows
Identical roofs
Like ordered army camps

There was a strange belief
That this was the only way
To make the north jealous

The problem was
That summer heat opened doors
And all the houses, head to tail
Were clear in the open sight

대마리49
— 파리 떼

사방을 둘러봐도
현무암 돌밭에다가
잡초뿐인 대마리 벌판에
파리들이 사는 것을
불가사의한 일이었다

음식 냄새만 나면
한두 마리가 아니라
새까맣게 몰려드는
파리 떼들은
어디에다 알을 낳고
구더기로 자라는지
알 수가 없었다

파리 떼들을 볼 때마다
난리 통에 죽은 시체들이
대마리 벌판 어디서
아직도 썩고 있는 것 같다는
상상도 했지만

사람들은 전쟁에서
죽은 중공군과 인민군들이
파리로 변한 것이라 했다

물론 북쪽에서는
미군, 국방군이 죽은 것이라
생각을 하고 있을 것이다

Daemari 49

Flock of Flies

All around, nothing but
a field of basalt rock
and weeds in this Daemari field
that a flock of flies lived here
was a mystery

With the smell of food
not one or two
but a black swarm
of flies descended
where they lay their eggs
to grow into maggots
was unknown

Upon a flock of flies
dead bodies ravaged by the war
seem still to be rotting
somewhere in this Daemari field
or so is imagined

People say, dead from the war

Chinese Reds and North Korean troops
had turned into flies

Of course, up north it'd be
US and South Korean troops
presumed dead and turned

대마리50
— 첫 모내기

개간 작업을 하면서도
물이 드는 무논에다
못자리를 설치한 것이
주접을 떨지 않고 자라
아카시아 향기 짙은 날
개간은 포기하고 모내기를 했다

허벅지까지 빠지는
두어 마지기 논에서
허우적거리며 모를 꽂을 때
오랜만에 피 냄새를 맡고
달려드는 거머리들

손등에 붙은 것은 떼어내고
종아리에 붙은 것은 털어내느라
정신이 없으면서도
온 신경은 흙속에 맨발에 쏠렸다

길쭉한 것이 밟히면

나무통이나 사람 뻐라 안심되고
딱딱한 것이 닿으면
혹시 지뢰가 아닐까
소스라치게 놀라면서
겨우겨우 마친 모내기

그해 가을 대마리 들판에서
백미 여덟 가마를 첫 수확했다

Daemari 50

First Planting

While clearing the minefields
we established a rice seedbed
in watery paddy
And it grew up more and more
So on a day acacia flowers bloom
we began planting

Thigh-deep in water
In two or some majigi paddy field
When we were floundering while planting
searching for a meal of blood
leeches started attacking

We were busy getting rid of them
on the back of our hands
and on our calves
But we only cared about our bare feet in mud

If it was something long we are stepping on
we were relieved that
it would be a piece of wood or human bones

If it was something solid
we were so frightened that
it might be mine
Barely finished planting in that way

That fall, in Daemari fields
we gathered eight bags of white rice

대마리51
— 분실

"중대장님, 우리가 전투에 나가
죽으면 어떻게 처리 되나요"

사흘째 비상 대기 중이던
전직 육군 하사 출신
김씨가 심각하게 물었다

"정식 군인이 아니고
 공식적 입주한 것도 아니라서
 전사 처리는 어렵고

군부대에 지급한 총을 들고
전투에 나섰으니
민간인 사망이라고 할 수 없고..."

중대장과 개척민 모두
난감하게 생각을 하고 있을 때
누군가 툭 한 마디 던졌다

"동네 방위병들이
전사하면 분실이라고 한다는데
우리도 그렇게 처리되겠지"

정말 다행인 것은
개척 기간 동안
분실 사태는 벌어지지 않았다

Daemari 51

Missing

"Sir,
what happens to our bodies
should we lose our lives in the battlefield?"

Cautiously asked
the former staff sergeant Kim
who had been staying all alert
for three days in a row

"Neither are we enlisted soldiers
nor are we formal Daemari villagers
Out of the blue, I dare reckon
to be recognized as soldiers killed in action

Drawing guns given out by the troops
and dashing through the battlefield
Out of place, I dare reckon
to be recognized as lost civilians..."

In the midst of
the tangled thoughts

slipped in a few words out of nowhere

"They say the town reserves are missing
every time their lives are lost in blood,
So where else shall our corpses be
the lads will simply go missing, bud"

Lucky enough, as we were to find
not a single sign of "missing" flesh
along the journey of reclamation

대마리52
— 삼천 원짜리 발목 지뢰

대마리 벌판에는
개척민을 애타게 기다리는
지뢰 세 잡놈이 있었다

우선 M16 잡놈
밟으면 현장 즉사는 물론
서른 발자국 안에 사람들도
귀신 친구를 만드는데
제작비는 천 원짜리 여섯 장

두 번째 대전차 지뢰
사람은 해치지 않으면서
무서운 탱크를 단박에
날려버리는데
몸값은 일만 오천 원

그리고 마지막으로
평생 발목 없는
병신으로 만드는 M14

그 지뢰 생산비는
단돈 삼천 원

그렇다면 삼천 원 짜리 지뢰 때문에
평생 다리병신으로 보내야 하는
절망의 가격은 얼마일까

아무리 변명을 해도
대마리 들판에
싸구려 지뢰를 뿌린 놈들보다
더 잡놈들은
세상에 없을 듯하다

Daemari 52

Ankle Mine, $3

There were three mines of shit
in the plain of Daemari
earnestly waiting for reclaimers

First of all, M-16 of shit
It costs six dollars
to make people within a 30-step radius
friends of ghost
of course including who steps on it

Next, Anti-tank mine
It blows the tank away
without hurting people
with just
fifteen dollars

Lastly, M-14
With it, you can live your whole life
as an ankleless idiot
Three dollars
is enough

Then, how much it will cost
to despair
living a whole life as the disabled?

No matter how many excuses are made
nobody is worse than
assholes
who sprinkled cheapie mines
on the plain of Daemari

대마리53
— 찜찜한 소문

주말에 부식을 가지러
집에 왔는데
마누라가 이상한 말을 했다

어떤 사람들이
민통선 안 땅을 찾기 위해
이것저것 묻고 다니고 있다는
찜찜한 이야기를 했다

힘든 노동에 지친 사람들은
나라에서 시키는 대로
개간을 하고 있는데
무슨 헛소리냐 일축을 했다

군부대에서 준 총을 들고
지뢰밭을 개간했는데
땅 임자가 우리지 누구냐며
오히려 역정을 했다

집구석에서
애나 잘 보고 있으라고
소리를 지른 다음
그 핑계로 친구들에게
술타령 하러 갔다

술에 취해서 돌아오면서도
땅임자가 있다는 소리
이상하게 귀에 거슬리기도 했지만

대마리 땅의 임자가
우리가 아니라는 놈들은
모두 사기꾼이라
철석같이 믿고 또 믿었다

Daemari 53

Uncomfortable Rumor

On the weekend
when I came home to get food
my wife told me a strange story

It was an uncomfortable story that
some people
were asking around
to find their land in the civilian controlled area

Bullshit!
People, tired by hard labour
dismissed it
We are the men who cultivating the land
following the government's order

Being angry, instead, said
We turned the minefield into the useful land
holding the gun given by army
so we are the masters of the land
Who else can be?

Just stay inside the house
and take good care of the kid well
Yelling at her
I went out for drinking with friends
with that excuse

On the way back, drunk,
the rumor about, so-called, the real landowner
nagged at my ear

Nevertheless, I believed and believed firmly that
those who said
we were not the master of Daemari
were all frauds

대마리54
— 반쪽 집

정부에서 지어 준 집은
집 한 채를 반으로 나눠서
두 가족이 사는 구조였다

작은 방 두 개
부엌을 겸한 거실
열두 평도 안 되는 반쪽 집

정부가 지어 준 집이라
그저 황송하게
이사를 했던 집

그래도 겉보기에는
그럴듯한 파란 슬레이트집이라
초가집에 사는 사람들이 부러워하던 집

살림살이가 없어서
그럭저럭 살만은 했지만
옆집에서 부부 싸움이라도 하는 날에는

온갖 악다구니는 다 들어야 했던
정말로 방음이 안 되는 최신식 집

그래도 이상하지 않았던 것은
반쪽 난 나라에서는
반쪽 집이 딱 맞았기 때문이었다

Daemari 54

Half House

In the government provided houses
one house was split in half
and two families resided

Two small rooms
A living room doubling as a kitchen
A half house not even twelve pyeong

The house we just
moved into gratefully
since the government provided it

The house that was envied by those living in cottages
as from the outside
It was a sparkling slate house

The house that was livable
as there were no other options
but its non-soundproof modern style
that on the days the next door couple argued
made us hear all of their arguing

But it wasn't strange
as for a country split in half
a house split in half was appropriate

대마리55
— 사고 현장

같이 개척을 하던 사람 중에
지뢰 사고가 나면
말 그대로 생지옥이다

꽝하는 폭음이
들리면 사람들은 순간적으로
자기 다리를 본다
두 다리가 붙어 있으면
나는 아니다 안심을 하고
검은 연기가 치솟는
곳을 찾는다

연기에 휩싸인 사람 발바닥은
이백 톤도 넘는 바람이
뼈와 살점을 다 헤집어 놓아
종아리까지 너덜너덜해진 상태

사람들이 달려가서
해야 하는 일은

피투성이 다리에서
성한 곳을 찾아
단단히 조여 매는 것이다

피가 더 이상 나오지 않도록
땀에 젖은 러닝셔츠라도
찢어서 칭칭 동여매는 일이다

군인 지프차에 실려
병원에 도착을 하면
의사는 성한 다리 아랫부분을
다 잘라내고 꿰매기만 하면
응급처치는 끝이었다

그렇게 잘라 낸 살점들은
병원 쓰레기통에 버려졌고
대기실 의자에는 가족들만
막막하게 앉아 있을 뿐이었다

Daemari 55

the Scene of the Accident

If a mine explodes
among reclaimers
there opens literally a living hell

BANG!
When people hear a loud bang
eyes immediately seek their legs
If they're still attached
heart feel relieved
then eyes chase
after the black smoke

Soles of one's feet in smoke
are already swept by
200 tons of gust
Bones and flesh
ragged to the calves

What people should do
right away is to
find the undamaged

from the covered in blood
and tie tightly

For no more bleeding
tear off even underwear
and fasten it tightly

Arrived at hospital
on the military's jeep
doctor cut off all the damaged
and stitch the rest up
That's all for first aid

Amputated flesh
dumped to trash
family in waiting room
draws a long face, hopelessly

대마리56

— 입주식과 6천 평 약속

통제부 골짜기에서 개척을 한지
1년 4개월이 지나
홀아비 냄새가 풀풀 나는
텐트촌 생활을 끝내고
전략촌 입주식을 하게 됐다

오랜만에 아버지는
풀을 먹인 와이셔츠를 입었고
어머니는 새 옷을 꺼내 입고
묘장 국민학교 운동장에 모여
눈물이 나는 입주식을 가졌다

8월 땡볕 아래 서 있는 것쯤은
참을 수 있었고
오랜만에 찍어 바른 분가루가
땀에 젖어 얼룩이 진 것도
아낙들에게는 창피한 일이 아니었다

귀빈들 인삿말이

엿가락처럼 늘어진 것은
약간 흠이었지만

내무부 장관, 농림부 장관, 국방부 장관들이
약속이나 한 듯 입 모아 떠들던
땅 6천 평을 보장한다
이 말을 철썩같이 믿었던 입주민들은
손바닥이 깨져라 박수를 쳤다

Daemari 56

The Moving-in Ceremony
and the Promise of Six-thousand-pyeong

A year and four months
since pioneering in the Tongjebu Valley
No more life in the tent
Leaving behind the stink of sweat
The day of the moving-in ceremony came

Father dressed up
in a starched shirt
Mother put on a new dress
We all gathered up in the yard of Myojang elementary school
for a moving-in ceremony of tears

Standing under the searing august sun
was bearable
The powder staining by sweat
on the women's faces
was endurable

Sure the lagging greetings

of distinguished guests
were rather uncomfortable

But the Ministers of Home Affairs, Agriculture, and National Defence
promised in union
six-thousand-pyeong of land
The residents foolishly took this for real
and clapped hard till their palms broke

대마리57

— 나무꾼과 지뢰

"할아버지
오늘도 백마고지 앞산으로
나무 하러 가세요"

"그 곳에 가면 삭정이들이 많아
새집으로 이사를 왔지만
아직 농사를 짓지 못해 볏짚이 없으니
나무를 해다 땔 수밖에..."

"할아버지 그곳은
발목 지뢰가 많다는데요"

"내가 며칠에 한 번씩 가는데
아직까지는 괜찮은데..."

대마리 개천에서 빨래를 하던
여자들과 이야기를 주고받은
할아버지는 지게를 지고
백마고지 앞산으로 간 뒤에

여자들이 저녁밥을 지으려고
빨래를 챙겨들고 허리를 펴는 순간

백마고지 앞산에서는
꽝하는 소리가
비명처럼 들렸다

Daemari 57

Woodcutter and Landmine

"Sir,
are you going to the mountain in front of Baeng-
magoji
to chop wood again today"

"A lot of dead branches are there
I moved to a new house
but I can't supply enough rice straw here
since I couldn't start farming yet
I should gather and chop wood to burn…"

"But sir,
it is said that many toe poppers are there"

"I go there every few days
but it's okay so far…"

The older man chatted
with women doing laundry at Daemari brook
and then, after he took his A-frame carrier
forward into the mountain

at the very moment
the women gathered the laundry up and straightened their back
to go cook dinner

BOOM
from the mountain in front of Baengmagoji came the sound
like a scream

대마리58

— 생명수 용강천

집은 그럴듯하게 지었는데
상수도 시설은 애초 없었다
현무암 위에 지은 집이라
우물을 팔 수도 없었고
교회 옆에 작은 옹달샘이 전부였다

마을 사람들은
난리 통에 시체를 던져 버려
파리와 구더기가 들끓고
살점을 뜯어 먹어 살이 통통 오른
우렁이들이 득실거렸던
용강천 물을 길어다 먹었다

아침 저녁, 물지게로 퍼 날랐고
이내 빨래터가 만들어졌고
대남 방송이 지겨운 낮에는
조무래기들 수영을 했고
개똥벌레 빛이 영혼처럼 떠도는 밤이면
개간에 지친 어른들이 목욕을 했다

그렇게 용강천을 둥둥 떠다니던
시체 이야기들은 대마리 사람들
삶 속에서 지워졌다

비가 내려 용강천이 흙탕물 되면
일찍 물을 길어다
흙탕이 가라앉을 때까지 기다려
치미는 갈증을 달래기 위해 마셨고
밥을 해서 허기를 채웠다

Daemari 58

Life Giving Water, Yonggang Stream

Houses were built quite decently
but water supply wasn't there from the first
Since the houses were on basalt
digging a well was not enable
only the little spring beside the church was all there was to it

People of the village
drank water from Yonggang stream where
the bodies thrown in during the panic of the war
caused full of flies, maggots
and chubby pond snails
gnawing the human bodies

Every morning and night
water was drawn with Jige and
soon, laundry place was made
In the daytime when propaganda broadcasting annoyed us
it became a swimming pool for little kids
In the night time when fireflies floated like souls

it became a bath for elders tired of working

Just like that, the memory of dead bodies
floating on the water
was forgotten from Daemari people's life

On a rainy day
when Yonggang stream became muddy
they drew water little earlier
waited for the mud to be sunk
to drink it to slake thirst and
to cook rice to appease hunger

대마리59

— 대마리 종합병원

사람들이 사는 곳이라
응급 환자들이 생기지만
출입이 금지되는 밤이 되면
검문소 밖을 나가지 못했다

그래서 생각을 한 것이
위생병 출신 입주민에게
약을 파는 것을 허용한 일이었다

처음에는 약국에서
상자와 병에 든 것을 파는 정도였지만
이리저리 경험이 쌓이면서
약사처럼 조제해서 판매를 했고
나중에는 주사약을 사다
직접 놓아 주기도 했다

어느 날 밤에는
양수가 터진 산모와 가족이 들이닥쳐
애걸을 하는 바람에 에라 모르겠다

아기를 받아 냈다

이 돌팔이 약방은
나중에 생긴 보건 진료소에 밀려
역사 속으로 사라졌지만
사람들 마음에는 병을 잘 고치는
대마리 종합 병원으로 남아있다

Daemari 59

The Daemari Hospital

Being a village
we'd had our occasional emergencies
But at night, with the curfew
we could never go past the checkpoint

Thus one of our neighbors—
a retired medic
was allowed to sell drugs instead

At first, our pharmacist
sold things straight from their bottles and boxes
But later
he started to prepare drugs himself
and even administer shots

One night
a to-be-mother and her family broke in
Please deliver our baby, they said
He became her midwife on the spur of the moment

This impromptu pharmacy
soon enough became history
however
being quick with a cure
the villagers still remember it quite fondly

대마리60

— 장롱 속 신부

"10호 아저씨, 경운기 위에
장롱 속에 뭐가 들었어요."

"이불 한 채 들었는데..."

"밧줄 좀 풀고
문 좀 열어 보세요."

"열쇠를 잃어 버렸는데..."

대마리 초소 앞에서 새파란 이등병 초병과
불안한 표정의 청년 실랑이가 계속 되고 있는데

밖을 내다보던 초소장
대마리 일이라면 뉘 집에 숟가락 개수까지
속속들이 꿰고 있는 초소장

총각을 힐끗 보더니
경운기 장롱 속에

한 달 후에 결혼할 여자가 숨어 있다는 것을 알기나 한 듯
씩 웃으며 명령을 내린다

'야, 그냥 통과 시켜!"

그날 대마리 어느 집에서는
가마 대신 장롱을 타고 온
신부의 신혼 방이 차려졌다

Daemari 60

The Bride in the Wardrobe

"'Ey! What's in that wardrobe?"

"A blanket—"

"Let's have a look, then?"

"Lost the key, though—"

It was quite a scuffle,
at the checkpoint on the road into Daemari:
a young man versus an even younger private

The checkpoint manager, peering out
The checkpoint manager, who knows every nook and cranny
everything that happens in the Village

Glancing at the young man,
he must've known—
that it was no bedding that was in the wardrobe
He hollered

"Let them through!"

That day, in Daemari,
a new family had found its home
A wife and her husband
the wife that rode a wardrobe, not a palanquin

대마리61

— 땅 제비뽑기

"지금부터
땅 제비뽑기를 하겠습니다"

"이미 천 평씩 측량을 마친 땅은
농사짓기 좋은 곳
그렇지 못한 곳
아직 개간하지 못한 땅
이렇게 나누어져 있고
각 집에서는 두 배미씩
제비를 뽑아 육천 평입니다."

"지뢰 사고를 당한
사람들은 제비를 뽑지 않고
고를 수 있도록 했습니다"

좋은 땅을 뽑은 가족들은
얼싸안고 춤을 추었고
그렇지 못한 사람들은
한숨을 내쉬게 만들었던

해외 토픽 감이던 땅 제비뽑기

그런데,

자기 땅 육천 평이 생겼다는 기쁨도 잠시

대마리에는 좋은 땅이 없다는 것을 아는데

그리 오래 걸리지 않았다

Daemari 61

Drawing Land Allocation Lots

"Now the time has come
to draw lots"

"The land already measured in each thousand-py-
eong
is divided as
good one
not that good one
and wild one
Each family draws two stricts
so the total is six-thousand-pyeong"

"Those who suffered mine accidents
can choose the land
without drawing a lot"

Those who drew the good one
hugged each other and danced with joy
but those who did not
let out a deep sorrowful sigh
The land allocation was indeed the hottest issue of

Daemari

Though,
The joy of having own land didn't last long
It took only a minute to realize
there was no such thing as 'good' land in Daemari

대마리62
— 등기를 낼 수 없는 땅

땅 뽑기를 한 밤에는
내 논 서른 마지기가 생긴
기쁨에 밤을 꼬박 새웠다

새벽 일찍 가족을 앞세우고
땅 구경을 시킬 때는
밥을 안 먹어도 배가 불렀다
시절을 믿을 수 없으니
땅문서를 만드는 것이 최고라
등기소를 찾았더니

사무를 보는 주사라는 놈이
대마리는 등기를 낼 수 없어요
쌀쌀하게 쏘아붙이고
쳐다보지도 않아

주눅이 들어 다시 물으니
땅 임자가 따로 있다고
한심하다는 듯이

위 아래를 훑어본다

더 이상 묻지도 못하고
얼이 빠져 집으로 돌아오면서도
나라에서 지뢰밭 개간까지 시켰는데
땅 사기를 치겠느냐
철석같이 믿었다

Daemari 62

The Land We Cannot Register

In the night after allocation
I could not sleep
with the joy of having our own land

In the early morning
showing our land to the family
I felt full as if stuffing myself
Just to be sure
would rather making a land deed
I visited a registry office

The guy on the desk
It is not accepted to register the land of Daemari
said cynically
without any glance

Daunted, I asked once again
He glanced me down
with pathetic eyes
and said there was somebody else who owned the land

Couldn't asking any more
coming back home, embarrassed
We even cleared the minefield
The government would not deceive us, would it?
I entirely trusted the government

대마리63
— 국유지

"이 땅은 국유지라서
등기를 낼 수 없습니다."

"아니, 국방부에서 시켜서
지뢰밭을 개간했는데
이게 경우가 맞는 말이요?"

"그 얘기는 국방부에 가서 하시고
지금 농사짓는 땅은
국가 재산을 불법 점유한 것입니다"

"지난 입주식에서 내무부 장관이
땅 6천 평을 보장한다고..."

"내부무 장관 마음대로
국가 땅을 줄 수는 없고
우선 오 년 치 임대료를 내야
국유지를 살 수 있습니다."

개척을 시킨 사람도
책임지는 사람도 없다는 것을
너무 늦게 알아버린 대마리 사람들은
서슬퍼런 대한민국 정부가 시키는 대로 했다

임대료 5년 치를 한꺼번에 내는
눈물 나는 특혜와
해마다 땅값을 나누어 갚는
파격적 조건으로
자신들이 목숨 걸고 개간했던 땅을
구입하는 계약서에 도장을 찍었다

Daemari 63

The National Property

"This is national property.
You cannot register this land"

"What? We even cleared the minefield
for the demand of Ministry of National Defense
Does it make sense?"

"Argue it there
You are now illegally
occupying the national property"

"At the Move-in Ceremony
the Minister of Home Affiars guaranteed the land...."

"Even the Minister cannot do it
in his own authority
You can buy it
once you pay five-year rental fee"

Knowing too late there was no one

who made people reclaim the land
and was responsible for the reclamation
the poor villagers had to do what imperious government ordered

Accepting the sorrowful privilege
of paying five-year rental fee at once
and the unprecedented terms
of paying back the cost of land annually
they had to buy the land
they'd risked their lives

대마리64
— 적산지

못자리 준비를 마치고
터덜터덜 돌아와
담배를 찾아서 불을 붙이는데
양복쟁이가 문을 흔든다

"아저씨가 농사짓는 땅이
적산지인데요"

"그게 뭐요"

"일본 놈들이 버리고
간 땅이라는 것입니다"

"임자가 없는 땅이니
개간한 내가 주인 되는 것 아니요"

"그건 국가 소유지로
해동 공사에서 관리를 하고 있는데
임대료 내셔야 합니다"

"그럼 지뢰밭 개간을 한
우리 몫은 어디에 있는 것이오"

"저에게 묻지 마시고
개간 시킨 사람에게 따지세요"

말이 끝나기도 전에 양복쟁이는
이 달 말까지 안내면
과태료 붙는다는 적산지 고지서를
마루에 던져 놓고 가는데

차마 닫지 못하는 문 안으로
대마리 벌판 매운 황사가 밀려와서
코가 시큰거렸다

Daemari 64

Jeoksanji

After preparing the seedbed
I trudged back
and lighted a cigarette
when a man clad in suit rattled the door

"The land you are farming on
is Jeoksanji"

"What is that"

"It means the Japanese abandoned
the land when they left this country"

"So if it's no man's land
don't I get to own it as a reclaimer"

"It is national property
managed by Haedong Company
so you have to pay the rent"

"Then where is our share of land

who reclaimed the mindfield"

"Don't ask me,
go argue with someone who ordered it"

Before even finishing his words
the man clad in suit tossed the bill
on the floor and left:
it warned that you'd be fined
if you don't pay by the end of this month

Into the door I couldn't bear to close
a burning wind of Daemari dust rolled in
stinging my teary eyes

대마리65

— 나타난 땅임자

개인에게 땅을 분배하고
가슴 설레는 첫 모내기를
준비하던 5월 어느 날
논에 물을 대러 갔던
사람 하나가 사색이 되어
마을 회관으로 뛰어 들어 왔다

지주가 몰래 들어와
경작 금지 팻말을 세웠다는 것이다
측량 기사까지 데리고 와서
논두렁을 따라 금줄을 쳐 놓았다는 것이다

목숨 걸고 개척한 땅을
꼼짝없이 빼앗기게 되었으니
어쩌라는 말이냐
주먹이 깨져라 벽을 쳤다

모내기 준비를 하던 사람들이
소식을 듣고 모여들어도

대책이 있을 리가 없어
검문소를 찾아가서
지주와 측량 기사를 들여보낸 것을
따져도 모르는 일이라 면박만 받았다

국방부 항의를 하니
농사지을 권리만 주었을 뿐
소유권을 준 적이 없다는
기가 막힌 소리로 염장을 지르고

꼼짝없이 땅을 빼앗기게 된 사람들은
집집마다 없는 살림을 털어서
변호사를 살 돈 삼백만 원을 만들었다

Daemari 65

The Landowner's Appearance

One day in May
after everybody had received their share of land
they prepared for the first planting
Hearts fluttering in anticipation
but a person who'd gone to water the paddies
dashed into the town hall
with an ashen face

The landowners had come in secret
and raised a "No Farming" sign
They'd brought a surveyor
and roped off the boundaries
on the ridges between the paddies

The land we had cleared
at the risk of their lives
had been taken with no resistance
What could we have done
in frustration we struck the wall
as our fists bled and broke

The people who had been getting ready for the planting
even though they gathered after hearing the news
There was no way they'd have an effective course of action
when they went to the military checkpoint
to ask about how they'd let in the landowner and his surveyor
with only the words "We don't know anything even if you ask,"
They were rebuffed

So they brought the matter to the Ministry of Defense
but there they were told an absurd truth
that only the right to farm on the land was given
not the right to own it

The people who'd suddenly found their land stolen from underneath them
went house by house to shake down families for

money they didn't have

and mde the three million won to hire a lawyer

대마리66
— 빰 한 대

"000가 누구야!"
"저인데요"
"나쁜 땅 사기꾼 놈"

서른 살도 안 된 검찰 직원이
쉰 살의 주민 빰을
철썩 한 대 올려 붙였다

의정부 검찰청
출두 명령을 받고 간 주민은
이유도 모른 채
아들 뻘 직원에게
빰따귀를 맞아야 했다

나라에서 시키는 대로 개척을 했는데
왜 때리느냐 물어볼 수 없었다
지뢰 사고를 당하지 않은 죄 밖에 없는데
왜 맞아야 하는지 따질 수도 없었다

손자국이 난 빰이 창피한 것도 모르고
그동안 일어났던 일을 설명하고
지뢰밭 개간 때보다
더 긴장되는 검찰 조서를 받았다

잘 봐 달라 고개가 땅에 닿도록
어린 놈들에게 인사를 하고 나오다가
진짜 땅 사기를 당한 것이
자신들이라는 걸 너무 늦게 알았다

한 달 뒤에
벌금형 고지서가 날아왔고
첫 수확한 쌀을 팔아
민주 시민답게 성실하게 납부를 했다

Daemari 66

A Slap on the Cheek

"Who is 000!"
"It's me sir"
"You damn land-swindler"

The prosecution office worker, not even 30 years old
Smacked the cheek
Of a 50-year old villager

To Uijeongbu Public Prosecutors' Office
went the villager
Without knowing why
His cheek had to be smacked
By the worker barely his son's age

He couldn't ask why he got smacked
when All he did was cultivate the land like the government told
He couldn't even dare to ask why he was getting smacked
when All he did was luckily avoid the mine acci-

dent

not noticing the handprint on my face
I explained what happened
Went through an investigation
by far more tense than the minefield cultivation

Coming out the office
Begging and bowing to the youngers for mercy
It was too late when I realized that
we were the ones being swindled

After a month
A fine notice arrived
So I sold the newly harvested rice
as a civil citizen I paid the fine

대마리67
— 그래도 우리 땅

지금도 아찔한
8.18 도끼만행 사건이 났던 밤
개가 미친 듯이 짖어서 밖을 보니
완전 군장을 한 군인들이
개인 참호에 들어가
전쟁 개시 명령만 기다리고 있었다

마을 회관에는 살이 떨리는
전시 상황실이 차려지고
하루 종일 무전을 주고받는 소리

인근 대광리 군인 가족들이 피난했다는 소문
비상 식량 미숫가루를 빻는 방앗간이 쉴 틈이 없다는 소문
휴전선 부근 마을 사람들이 피난 보따리를 쌌다는 소문
동송 부잣집이 택시로 서울로 야반도주했다는 소문

그러나 대마리 주민들은 달랐다

참호에 대기 중인 군인들 전투 식량이
마른 건빵뿐이라는 이야기를 듣고
남자들은 집집마다 옥수수와 감자를 걷었고
여자들은 솥단지를 걸고 그것을 쪄서
하루 세끼 조달 하듯이
참호 속 군인들에게 전달을 했다

오르지, 배가 든든해야 전쟁을 이길 수 있다는 생각
대마리 땅은 절대로 빼앗길 수 없다는 오기 때문에
군인들보다 더 치열하게 전쟁 준비를 했었다

Daemari 67

Even So, It's Our Land

The dizzying night
of the August 18th axe incident
A dog was barking like mad
So I looked outside
Soldiers in full battle gear
had entered their individual trenches
awaiting only the order to begin war

At the town hall was set up
a bone-chilling wartime command post
All day the sound of radio, back and forth

The rumor that soldiers' families in nearby Dae-gwangri had evacuated
The rumor that the millers making the flour for emergency rations were working without rest
The rumor that the villages around the DMZ had packed for evacuation
The rumor that a rich family in Dongsong had fled to Seoul during the night

But the villagers of Daemari were different
After hearing that rations for those troops waiting in trenches
were nothing but dry hardtack
The men went house by house to collect corn and potatoes
The women took the pots and steamed the food the men collected
as if they were army chefs themselves
they delivered meals to the soldiers in the trenches

Knowing that wars are won on full stomachs
with the conviction that they would never
Lose the land of Daemari to any other
they prepared more intensely than any soldier

대마리68

— 백마고지 위령탑

"나라를 위해 싸운 군인들을
욕보이는 짓입니다."

"당장 도끼로 깨버리고
다시 세우세요."

관광객인 듯한 사람이
백마고지 위령탑에 근무 중인
장교 멱살을 잡고 악을 쓰고 있었다

"어떻게 침략자 중공군이
희생된 숫자를
비문에 새겨 넣을 수 있어..."

"살아서도 원수는
죽어서도 불구대천 원수인데..."

대마리 사람들이
입주식을 할 때마다

희생자 추모 제례를 해서
백마고지 위령비가 세워졌는데

관광을 온 사람이
말이 되는 것 같기도 하고
안 되는 것 같은 소리로
하루 종일 따지고 또 물고 늘어졌다

그 사건 이후 공들여 세운
위령 비문은 정말로 깨져 나갔고
중공군 숫자가 없는
맞춤식 비문이 다시 세워졌다

Daemari 68

Baengmagoji Memorial

"It's a dishonor
on the soldiers who fought for our country"

"Break it with ax right away
and remake it"

A man looked like a tourist
yelled and grabbed the officer's throat
who guarded the memorial

"How could you carve the number of casualties
among the Chinese invaders
on the memorial…"

"Once an enemy, forever an enemy.
Even if we are dead…"

Baengmagoji memorial was raised
due to Daemari people who held
the memorial ceremony for victims
every time they celebrated settlement

A tourist
argued all day long
with words seemed to make sense
or to make no sense

After that
the memorial stone really was broken and re-
moved
and a new special memorial was raised again
without the number of Chinese soldiers

대마리69
— 나물 뜯기

“형님, 나물 뜯으러 가요.”

“바쁜 못자리를 끝냈으니
나물 뜯으러 가요.”

“야산에 봄나물들이
낫으로 베야 할 정도로 많아요.”

“내가 며칠 다녀 보니
지뢰는 없는 것 같아요.”

처음에는 논두렁 끝자락에
드문드문 올라오는 고사리를
재미 삼아 꺾어 말리던 것이

점점 낮은 산으로 가고
그것도 없어지자
산으로 한 발 한 발 들어갔다

산자락을 오를 때마다
나물 보따리는
점점 무거워졌고

처음에는 지뢰가 덜컥 겁이 났지만
몇 번 나물을 뜯다 보니
지뢰가 있다는 것이
정말 거짓말 같았다
동생이 그 산길에서
지뢰 사고로 죽기 전 까지는

Daemari 69

Picking Wild Herbs

"Mrs. Lee, let's go to pick some wild herbs"

"Now that we finished busy funerals,
let's go to pick some wild herbs"

"There are so many spring herbs in the hill
that they have to be cut with sickles"

"I've been there for a few days,
there's no mine"

at first we just picked
and dried some bracken
which is coming up at the edge of the rice paddy

but we began to walk into the hills
and when all of the bracken was picked
we began to walk into the mountains

the more we went up the mountain
the heavier

our herb bag became

at first, we were afraid of the mine
but as time goes by
it felt like a lie
that there were mines
Before my brother died
in a mine accident

대마리70

— 의족

"지뢰를 밟은 상황에 대해서
조금 더 자세히 말씀해 주세요."

진실보다는 호기심뿐인
방송국 기자들이 찾아와서
언제나 하는 말이다

그런데 지뢰를 밟은 순간은
전혀 기억이 나지 않는다
다만 정신을 잃고 난 뒤에
깨어나니 다리 하나가 없어졌다는 것

그것이 전부였다

의족을 벗어
그럴듯하게 세워 놓고
살점이 말라 뭉툭해진 다리를
카메라에 담고 방송이 나온 다음에는

객지로 나간 자식들이
전화를 해서
쓸데없는 짓을 했다고 타박을 하지만

마을 사람들도
괜히 동네 이미지만 떨어진다고
투덜거리며 눈총도 주지만

우리가 카메라에
발가벗는 마음으로 의족을
보여야 하는 이유는 단 한 가지

우리를 지뢰밭 안으로 밀어 넣고
모르쇠 하는 사람들 양심에
이렇게라도 호소하기 싶기 때문이다

Daemari 70

Prosthetic Leg

"Please be more specific about the time
When you stepped on a land mine"

What reporters always say
only with curiosity
rather than seeking truth

I do not remember
the moment I stepped on the landmine
Yet after a blackout
I woke up with only one leg

Lowering my head like a sinner
I came back home with a limp walking on crutch-
es
that wife got from somewhere
That's all I remember

When we took off prosthetic leg
and put it decently

our legs
now stumpy with dried flesh are
captured by camera and then broadcasted

Then
call from children
who live away from home
ragging
for doing useless things

Then
glare from other villagers
grumbling
It would only degrade town's reputation for noth-
ing

Still
one and only reason
why we show our legs in front of camera
feeling naked

It’s the only way to appeal to conscience of people
who rammed us in the minefield
and pretend to not know

대마리71
— 등화관제

낮에는 전략촌이라고
자랑을 하다가도
밤이 되면 불빛을 가렸다

북한에서 불빛을 보고
총을 쏠까 봐
아니면 길을 잃은 간첩들이
숨어들어 오는 것을 막기 위해
등화관제를 철저히 했다

요즘은 블라인드가 있지만
그 시절에는 귀한 군용 담요로
창문을 가려야 했다

해가 떨어지면
불빛이 새어 나갈까 봐
사람들이 밖으로 다니지 않아
버려진 도시 같았다

보름달이 뜨는 밤이면
똑같이 지은 집들이
줄줄이 서있는 모습은
정말로 기괴했다

잘못해서 불빛이 새어 나가면
군부대에서 비상 전화가 오고
리 사무실에서는 방송을 했다

그래도 불빛이 가려지지 않으면
무장을 한 군인들이
득달 같이 찾아와서
방문을 흔들어 댔다

Daemari 71

Blackout

During the day
we bragged about it as a strategic village
but at night we covered up the lights

In order to prevent
the North from shooting
or the lost spies
from entering the village
the blackout was strictly enforced

There are blinds these days
but in those days, we had to cover the windows
with precious military blankets

It was like an abandoned city
because people were afraid that the lights would leak out
they didn't go out at all
when the sun went down

On a full moon night

it was really bizarre
to see a row of houses
built in the same way

If the lights leaked out by mistake
the military unit called for an emergency
and ri-office warned

But if the lights still weren't out
armed soldiers
immediately came
and shook the door

대마리72

— 아내들에게 바치는 헌시

솔직히 말을 해서
대마리 땅의 절반은
남편을 잘못 만난 아내들의
눈물과 한숨으로 만든 것이네

남편을 지뢰밭으로 보내고
철조망 방석에 앉은 마음으로
북쪽에서 퐁소리만 들려도
의무대 차량이 나오는 것만 봐도
손끝이 떨려서 아무 것도 못했다던 당신

땅을 분배받은 새벽
아침밥을 준비하면서도
우리 땅이 있는 곳을
바라보면서 미소 짓던 당신

남편보다 먼저 나가서
버드나무 뿌리를 뽑았고
지뢰를 발견하면 아무렇지도 않게

캐내서 집어 던지던 당신

첫 수확을 하던
화지리 방앗간에서
방금 나온 흰쌀을
두 손으로 꼭 움켜쥐고
뜨거운 눈물을 떨구던 당신

어느 날, 땅임자라고 나선
남자 멱살을 틀어쥐고

"우리 땅은 절대로
빼앗길 수 없다"

피를 토하듯 외치던
대마리의 진정한 주인 당신

Daemari 72

The Poem for Our Wives

To be honest
the half of Daemari
was built upon by the tears and sighs of
those women who married poverty

You
left behind husbands in a minefield
with heavy hearts as if sitting on barbed wire
when an echo of artillery from the North was heard
when an ambulance of medical detachment was seen
you could do nothing with trembling hands

You
in the dawn after the land allotment
even while preparing breakfast
you looked at the land, our land
and silently smiled

You

went out earlier than your husband
then pulled out willow roots
and when finding mines
you dug them up and threw them away
without any blink

You after harvesting for the first time
wept hot tears
clasping the pure-white rice polished
just now at Hwajiri mill

One day, seizing a man by his collar tightly
who claimed the land ownership

"Nobody can take away our land, never!"
You, shrieked as if coughing up blood

The true heroines of Daemari
Our wives

대마리73

— 팔뚝질 논

대마리 근처에서 벼 베기를 하던
화지리 사람들 이야기 중에
팔뚝질 논이 있다

낫으로 벼를 베던 시절
마침 그 위를 지나가던
별을 단 헬기가 있어서
장난기 심한 사람이
못 보겠지 하고 팔뚝질을 했다

그런데 잘 가던 헬기가
다시 돌아와
어른 키보다 약간 높게
논 위를 한 바퀴 돌았고
바람 날벼락을 맞은 사람들은
논바닥에 납작 엎드려
두 손을 모아 빌었다

헬기가 화풀이를 하고 간 논에

베어놓았던 벼들이
사방팔방으로 날아갔고
나머지 벼들도
헬기에 탄 사람 마음처럼 배배 꼬여서
일꾼 열명을 사서 사흘 동안
헬기 설거지를 했었다

이 말을 들은 대마리 사람들은
헬기가 요란스럽게 지나갈 때
더러 켈로 부대 출신은
거수경례를 올려붙이기는 했지만
하늘을 날아가는 잠자리 보듯
대부분 아는 체를 하지 않았다

Daemari 73

Fields of Raised Fist

There's a story about fields of raised fist
told by Hwajiri people
who had reaped rice near Daemari

At the times that people reaped rice with scythe
a wicked man raised fist
to the star-marked helicopter
flying above the fields,
thought they could not see him

But the helicopter
returned from its way
made a circle above the fields
at the level only a little higher than an adult's height
People hit by a storm out of the blue
begged with both hands
lying down flat on the ground

After the helicopter vented its anger,
reaped rice plants were scattered everywhere

and the rest were tangled
like the feelings of the pilot
So they needed to hire a hand
to wash the helicopter's dishes for three days

Being told this story,
when a helicopter passed by noisily
although those people who used to be in KLO Unit
made a salute to the helicopter
Daemari people mostly ignored it
as if it was just a dragonfly in the sky

대마리74
— 수류탄으로 우물 파기

"아저씨, 목책에 부비 트랩으로 걸어 놓은
수류탄 좀 떼어 가지 마세요."

군인들이 사정을 했지만
곰보돌을 깨고 우물을 파야 하는
주민들에게는 소귀에 경 읽기였다

우물을 파내려 가다 곡괭이 날이 휘는
단단한 암반이 나오면
구멍을 뚫어 수류탄을 넣고
연결한 도화선에 불을 붙였다

줄을 잡고 올라오다
잘못해서 떨어지면
폭사를 하는
세상에서 가장 미련했던
수류탄으로 우물 파기

폭발한 암반이 주변 민가로 튀는 것을

막기 위해 버드나무 가지를 잘라
삐삐선으로 엮어 만든 멍석을
우물 위에 덮으면서
귀가 멍멍해지도록
수류탄 폭발 소리를 들으며
한 자 한 자 파내려 가는 공사를 하는 날에는

폭음을 듣고
현장으로 달려 온
군인들도 우물을 들여다보면서
물이 나오지 않는 것에
혀를 끌끌 차고 되돌아갔다

Daemari 74

Digging Wells with Grenades

"Sir, please stop taking
the grenades we set up as booby traps."

The soldiers pleas to the villagers
who had to dig wells through rock
fell upon deaf ears

While digging a well
if some bedrock stopped the pick
they'd bore a hole into the rock
drop in a grenade
and set fire to its fuse

While climbing back up the hole
if they slipped and fell
they'd be blown apart
The world's most foolish task
digging wells with grenades

To stop shrapnel from being flung into nearby houses

they'd make nets with willow branches
tied together with electric cable
and drape them over the well
On these days where they dug, foot by foot
ears ringing from the bombs' blasts

The soldiers who'd rush over
at the sound of explosions
would peer into the well
Seeing no water
they'd cluck their tongues
and return to their posts

대마리(최종)

— 개척비

마을 중간에
한탄강 화강암으로 만든
그동안의 역사를 새긴
개척비가 서 있다

짤막한 비문에
허망한 기록을 담았고
죽음을 같이 했던 동지들
이름 하나하나가 새겨져 있다

언제나 그렇듯
세월의 매서운 바람이
찾는 사람 없는 비문을 긁어서
점점 희미해져 갈 것이고
사람들은 대마리 개척 역사를
지난 이야기로 생각할 것이다

그렇다고 해서
지옥보다 더 절망스러운 땅에

개척이라는 이름으로
순진한 사람을 밀어 넣었던
무책임한 군부대의 욕심

6천 평의 약속을 외면했던
대한민국의 거짓말을
덮을 수는 없다

지뢰에 끊어진 발목에서
흐르는 뜨거운 피를 움켜쥐고
병원으로 가는 지프차가
오기를 기다리던
핏방울 맺힌 눈동자를
대마리 하늘과 들판은
똑똑히 기억할 것이다.

Daemari 75

The Epitaph

Middle of the village
there stands an epitaph
made of granite from Hantan River
telling the chronicles of the village

The short inscription
contains forlorn memories
and the name of comrades
who suffered the same fate

As always
time passes
and the epitaph, nobody visits
is weathered by bleak wind
and reclamation of Daemari
is regarded as an old story

Nevertheless
Memories will never be forgotten:
the rapacity of irresponsible army
which hustled innocent people to hopeless, barren

land
under the name of reclamation

and the deceitful government
which forsook the promise
of the land, six-thousand pyeong

The sky and the land of Daemari
will never forget
the resentful, red eyes
wrapping the ankle
spilling hot blood
severed by mine
waiting for the jeep
to the hospital

해설

시인의 역할, 시의 효용성

—정춘근의 시로 쓴『지뢰꽃 마을, 대마리』역사

이영춘(시인)

1. 지뢰꽃 시인

여기 특별한 한 시인을 만난다. 그 시인은 철원 출신으로 철원을 지키고 있는 정춘근 시인이다. 그는 이미 1999년『실천문학』봄호에 등단작이기도 한 〈지뢰꽃〉으로 널리 알려진 시인이다. '지뢰꽃'이란 제목만으로도 암시되듯 수복지구에 전쟁의 상흔으로 남아 있는 '지뢰'를 소재로 하여 쓴 작품이다. 우선 그의 등단작 〈지뢰꽃〉 이란 작품부터 다시 새겨 보아야 할 필요성이 요구된다.

월하리를 지나/대마리 가는 길/철조망 지뢰밭에서는/가을꽃이 피고 있다//지천으로 흔한/지뢰를 지긋이 밟고/제 이념에 맞는 얼굴로 피고 지는/이름 없는 꽃/꺾으면 발밑에/뇌관이 일시에 터져/화약 냄새를 풍길 것 같은 꽃들//저 꽃의 씨앗들은/어떤 지뢰 위에서/뿌리내리고/가시철망에 찢긴 가슴으로/꽃을 피워야 하는

걸까//흘깃 스쳐 가는/병사들 몸에서도/꽃 냄새가 난다//
(「지뢰꽃」) 전문

상상만으로도 그 땅에 무수히 많은 지뢰가 묻혀 있음이 암시된다. 산천에 피어 있는 꽃들이 전부 '지뢰밭'이 된 폭발물 위에서 꽃을 피워낸 것이다. 이 '지뢰꽃'은 전쟁에서 목숨 잃은 영혼들의 넋으로 상징되기도 한다. 무심히 흘러가는 계절과 시간 속에서 그들의 넋은 잠들 수 없어 꽃으로 승화된 것이다. 더구나 이 시의 핵심 사상은 "지뢰를 지그시 밟고/제 이념에 맞는 얼굴로 피고 지는/이름 없는 꽃"이라고 시인은 형상화 하고 있다.

어찌 보면 이번 시집 『지뢰꽃 마을 대마리』는 그의 첫 시집 『지뢰꽃』의 후속편에 속한다고 할 수 있다.

정춘근 시인이 끊임없이 추구하는 사실성을 바탕으로 한 역사성이 이번 시집에서도 면면이 나타나고 있기 때문이다. 그러므로 이 시집은 그 현장감이 더욱 생생하게 인식되고 재현된다.

그는 이번 시집 『지뢰꽃 마을 대마리』에서 그의 시적 발화와 주제를 이렇게 밝히고 있다.

"이 시는 한국 전쟁 당시 버려진 땅을 농경지로 사용하기 위해 출신 성분이 좋은 150명을 선발해서 군 부대장 지휘 아래 지뢰밭을 개간했던 이야기다. 당시 계곡 사이에 텐트를 치고 직접 만든 탐지기로 지뢰를 제거하는 작업을 하면서 10%에 해당하는 사람들이 지뢰 사고를 당해 현장에서 사망하였다. 그렇게 개간한 땅은 나중에 땅 주인이 나타나서 빼앗기거나 돈을 주고 사야 했던 분단의 그늘 아래서 벌어졌던 숨겨진 아픈 역사다."라고 설명한다.

우리는 여기서 역사란 과연 무엇인가를 다시 한번 생각하게 된다. 영국의 역사학자 에드워드 핼릿 카(Edwrd Hallett Carr)의 역사란 무엇인가? (What Is History)(1961)에서 그는 이렇게 정의한다. "역사란 역사가와 그의 사실들의 끊임없는 상호 작용하는 과정, 즉 현재와 과거 사이의 끊임없는 대화"라고 했다. 그는 '대화'에 대한 설명으로 "대화의 주체는 개인이 아니며 당시 사회와 오늘의 사회 간의 대화이며 더 나아가 역사란 과거의 사건들과 서서히 등장하고 있는 미래의 목적들 사이의 대화"라고 정의한다. 이런 의미망의 연결로 볼 때 정춘근은 "현재와 과거 사이의 끊임없는 대화"를 하고 있는 시인이다. 그의 제1 시집 『지뢰꽃』에 이어 이번 시집 『지뢰꽃 마을 대마리』도 그에 의해 우리 민족 수난의 역사적 대화는 계속 되고 있는 것이다. 이제부터 정춘근 시인의 언어를 통하여, 우리 민족 수난의 역사를 그의 "칼보다 무서운 펜"을 통하여 그 현장을 살펴보자.

2.시인의 역사의식

정춘근 시인의 일곱 번째 시집 『지뢰꽃 마을 대마리』의 배경은 강원도 철원군 철원읍에 위치한 지명이다.

시인은 한국 전쟁, 즉 6.25를 직접 겪지 않은 세대이다. 그러나 자신이 탄생하고 성장한 고장에서, 그 참혹한 전쟁의 상흔으로 폐허가 된 땅에서, 일어난 사건들을 보고 듣고 겪은 전설 같은 이야기들을 시로 승화시켜 낸 것이다. 지뢰밭 속에서, 목숨을 담보로 해야 하는 땅에서, 아버지 혹은 삼촌 같은 분들이 살기 위해, 밥을 위해, 그 위험한 땅을 농경지로 개척해 가는 과정에서 벌어지는 각종 사고와 핍박을 당하는 민초들의 이야기다.

E.H. 카Carr의 역사에 대한 정의와 같이 정춘근 시인은 그 자신이 "과거의 사실과 현재의 역사가로 대화"를 하고 있는 것이다. 라이너 마리아 릴케는 말한다. "시는 체험이다"라고.

분단 접경지역에서 나고 자란 한 시인으로서 그곳에서 일어난 사건의 질곡한, 그리고 애절한 역사의 고증 같은 시詩를 승화시켜 낸 작품이기에 더욱 값진 자산으로 평가된다. 생과 사의 갈림길에서 목숨을 담보로 삶의 현장을 개척해 가는 개척민들의 역사적 면면이 너무나 생생하게 그려져 있어 큰 울림을 준다.

이제 그의 시집 『지뢰꽃 마을 대마리』의 내용을 몇 개의 특성으로 분류하여 단계별 진행 순서를 따라가면서 살펴보았다. 그 특성을 현장성(역사성), 생명성, 문학성으로 분류해 보았다. 첫째, 현장성은 사실을 바탕으로 진술한 시적 장치다. 그러므로 현장성은 곧 역사성으로도 대치된다. 둘째, 생명성은 생명 존중 사상이다. 비무장 지대에서 죽은 영혼들을 '지뢰꽃'으로 승화한 것 자체가 생명의 부활이다. 또한 개척민들의 인간 이하의 삶과 노동의 착취, 그리고 목숨을 담보로 하는 민초들의 생生에 초점을 맞춘 주제 의식 또한 생명 존중 사상으로 간주된다. 셋째, 문학성은 시집『지뢰꽃 마을 대마리』에 나타난 그의 작품성이다. 이 시의 특성인 '역사성'에 초점을 맞추다보면 자칫 문학성을 소홀이 할 수도 있다. 그러나 정춘근 시인은 작품마다 주제 의식과 예술의 본령인 정서(emotion)에 초점을 맞춰 시의 고결성을 승화시켜 내고 있다.

이렇게 정춘근 시인은 수복지구 '대마리'에서 일어난 사건과 사실을 바탕으로 고증하듯 순행적 전개 과정을 밟아가며 시로써 역사를 증명하고 있다. 지뢰밭을 농경지로 개간한다는 소문에서부터 출발하여 목숨을 잃고 불구가 되면서 개척한 땅을 빼앗기는 장면까지 세세히 묘사되어 있어 가슴을 뭉클하게 한다. 그 중에도 현장감이 두드러진 몇 작품을 예로 들어보겠다.

> "땅 서른 마지기를 준단다."/"그것도 공짜로 나눠 준단다."//긴가민가한 소문이/수복지구를 떠돌았다. 〈대마리1.-서른 마지기 소문〉1.2연

> 대마리 개척단/이름은 전략촌이었다.

순찰을 하던 사단장이/황무지로 버려진 대마리를/평소에는 개간을 하다가/전투가 벌어지면 바로/총을 들고 나서 싸우는/이스라엘 기브츠 비슷한 구조를 만들면/땅도 얻고 전투력도 얻고/꿩 먹고 알 먹고 생각에/만들어진 전략촌이었다 〈대마리4.-전략촌〉1.3연

군대를 제대한 사람/나이는 마흔 이하/식구는 네 명 이하/재산이 10만 원 넘어도 탈락/사상이 건전한 사람/행정 기관 추천 도장을 꽝 받아서/근엄한 선발 위원회를 통과한 사람 〈대마리5.-신청 조건〉3연

지뢰가 묻힌 지옥 같은 땅, 그곳에 '전략촌'이 생긴 다는 소문이 시의 발화점이 되어 있다. (「대마리2」)에서 소문이 사실로 증명된다. 그리고 까다로운 신청 조건이 (「대마리5.」)와 같이 전제된다. "군대를 제대한 사람/나이는 마흔 이하"이다. 청장년층의 노동력을 염두에 둔 선발이다. 분단국가의 비극을 암시하듯 "사상이 건전한 사람"이라야 한단다. 또한 민초들의 삶을 암시하는, "재산이 10만 원 넘어도 탈락"이란다. 비참을 넘어 생生에 대한 회의마저 불러일으킨다.

입주증을 발급 받기 전에/기가 막힌 각서를 썼다/군부대 지시에 잘 따르고/개간하는 과정은 일급비밀/그리고 지뢰사고로 죽어도 좋다는/요즘 말로 표현 하자면/신체 포기

각서를 썼다. 〈대마리6.-입주증〉3연

전략촌으로 가는 날/다시 만날 기약 없는 가족들과/아침을 먹는 둥 마는 둥/남자들은 연장을 챙겨 들고/대마리로 갈 채비를 했다 〈대마리7.-가입주〉3연

장군들도 별판을 가리고 가야 하는/먼지 풀풀 날리는 신작로를 지날 때/쟁쟁하게 들리던 대담방송은/ 마치 환영을 하는 소리 같았다 〈대마리7-가입주〉5연

전쟁의 상흔으로 존재하는 땅, 그 땅의 역사는 이렇게 흘러가야만 하는 것인가? 상상만으로는 가늠이 안 되는 역사의 현장이다. (「대마리6」)에서 '입주증' 각서는 "지뢰 사고로 죽어도 좋다는/신체 포기 각서를 썼다"는 것이다. 사십 미만의 젊은이들의 "신체 포기 각서"이다. 산다는 것, 먹고 산다는 것이 과연 무엇일까를 사유케 한다. 그것도 (「대마리7」)에서 나타나 있듯이 완전 입주가 아니라, 가 입주다. "전략촌으로 가는 날/다시 만날 기약 없는 가족들과"의 이별이다. 입주 후에도 그 전략촌에서 식사도 스스로 해결해야 했다. "먹을 식량과/간장 된장을 챙겨 넣고" (「대마리7」) 지뢰밭을 향하는 것이다. 그리고 그곳에는 아직도 전사한 영혼들의 아우성 같은 "대남 방송이/마치 환영을 하는 소리 같이" 들리고 있는 곳이다.

우선, 독자 행동은 금물/굴비처럼 열 명씩 다니기 위해/아는 사람들 끼리 조를 짰고/단 일주일 치 식량이/선물처럼 배급됐다. 〈대마리8.-통제부 골짜기〉1.5연

(「대마리8」)은 접경 지대의 살벌한 분위기와 개척민들의 행동지침이 잘 그려져 있다."북한군 저격 때문에/별판을 가리고 다녀야"만 하는 북한과의 대척 지역이다. 그리고 "독자 행동은 금물/굴비처럼 열 명씩 다녀"야만 하는 곳이다. 그리고 그곳에서의 의. 식. 주, 문제는 가히 상상을 초월한다. "때에 찌든 검은 솥을 걸고 /시금털털한 김치도 넣고/푸석 말라비틀어진 시레기도 넣고/ 먹다 남은 멸치 대가리도 넣고/---감자, 된장, 고추장, 썩을 놈의 세상도/다 풀어 넣고 끓이다가/마지막에 국수, 칼국수/가리지 않고 집어넣는다"(「대마리19」)에서 진술하고 있는 개척민들의 식사, "털레기 국수"인 것이다. 잠자리 또한 말이 아니다.

신병들처럼 고된 훈련이 끝나고 "잠자리에 들려고 보면/텐트 안은 흙바닥이라/뼛속을 파고드는 냉기를 막으려고/버드나무를 잘라서 얼기설기 펼쳐 놓고/그 위에서/새우잠을 청한다"(「대마리9」)라고 진술한다.

인간이 위기에 처했을 때 가장 먼저 찾는 것은 무엇일까? 인류 공통분모의 하나로 그것은 '신 神'이라고 한다. 이 '전략촌'에 입소된 개척민들도 아마 그런 심정이었던가 보다.

지뢰를 밟아도/뇌관이 고장 나서 터지지 않게 해 주시고/

자꾸만 집으로 돌아가고 싶어지는/ 갈대 같은 마음이 흔들리지 않게/꼭꼭 잡아 주시고 〈대마리10.-산신제〉3연

"평생 神神을 찾지 않던 사람들도/오늘 만큼은 공손히 머리를 조아리고/산신제 막걸리 잔을 올렸다"고 진술한다. 그러나 지뢰사고는 일어났고, 보상금은 0원이었다.(「대마리26-지뢰사고 보상금 0원」). 이 역사의 현장은 참혹하다 못해 끔찍하다. (「대마리31-지푸라기 다리」)란 작품에서 그 실상을 보자.

지뢰 사고로 다리 잘려 죽은 친구를/그냥 장사를 지낼 수가 없어/의족을 만들어 초상을 치뤘다//하늘 나라에 가서도/다리 병신 취급 받을 것 같아/지푸라기로 만든 다리를/그럴싸하게 달아매었다//--- ---

사람 썩는 냄새로/고개가 절로 돌아가는/지푸라기 다리를 붙일 때/흐르는 땀 속에 섞였던 눈물을/누가 기억이나 할까//미처 감지 못한 두 눈빛이/무섭고 애처로워 다시 쓸어내려 주고/서둘러 나올 때/여보게 부르는 소리가 들리는 듯/자꾸만 돌아보게 되는/절망을 그 누가 알고 있을까 〈대마리31-지푸라기 다리〉3행 빼고 전문

이런 죽음 앞에, 목숨 앞에 더 이상 무슨 말이 필요하겠는가! 화자의 표현 대로 "자꾸만 돌아보게 되는" 심상의 처절함뿐이다. "그렇게 잘라 낸 살점들은/병원 쓰레기통에

버려졌고/대기실 의자에는 가족들만/막막하게 앉아 있을 뿐이었다"(「대마리55-사고 현장」)고 암흑 같은 참상을 시인은 첨예하게 그려내고 있다. 이렇게 목숨을 잃어가며 개간한 땅은 어떻게 되었는가! (「대마리56」)입주식애서는 개척민들에게 이렇게 약속한다.

내무부 장관, 농림부 장관, 국방부 장관들이/약속이나 한 듯 입 모아 떠들던/땅 6천 평을 보장한다

〈대마리56-입주식과 6천평 약속〉 5연 부분

그러나 이런 약속은 어디로 갔는가? "이 땅은 국유지라서/등기를 낼 수 없습니다." "아니, 국방부에서 시켜서/지뢰밭을 개간했는데---" "그런 얘기는 국방부에 가서 하시고/지금 농사짓는 땅은/국가 재산을 불법 점유한 것입니다"(「대마리63」) 이런 날벼락 같은 대답만 돌아온 것이다. 결국 개척민들은 자신들이 개간한 땅을 구입해야만 하는 참상이 벌어진 것이다. 넌센스다.

임대료 5년 치를 한꺼번에 내는/눈물 나는 특혜와/해마다 땅값을 나누어 갚는/파격적 조건으로/자신들이 목숨을 걸고 개간했던 땅을/구입하는 계약서에 도장을 찍었다 〈대마리63-국유지〉7연

역사적 사건의 흐름과 개척민들의 실상의 면면을 보기 위하여 몇 작품을 더 부분적으로 인용한다.

"꼼짝없이 땅을 빼앗기게 된 사람들은/집집마다 없는 살림을 털어서/변호사를 살 돈 삼백만 원을 만들었다"(「대마리65-나타난 땅 임자」)

"000가 누구야!"/"저인데요"/"나쁜 땅 사기꾼 놈"//서른 살도 안 된 검찰 직원이/쉰 살의 주민 뺨을/철썩 한 대 올려붙였다 〈대마리66-뺨 한 대〉1.2연

이렇게 개척민들은 개간한 땅을 빼앗기고 인권을 유린당하는 수난과 수모를 겪었다. 이것이 오늘날 비무장 지대의 역사다. 역사는 이렇게 피 흘린 땅 위에 세워지는 것인가? 무엇보다 그 장대한 이야기를 시로 승화시켜 낸 시인의 저력을 주의 깊게 주목할 필요가 있다.

시는 정서를 바탕으로 하여 승화되고 이미지화되는 것에서 그 가치가 발휘된다. 시인의 『지뢰꽃 마을 대마리』는 편편마다 "시는 수학이다."라고 한 장 콕토의 정의대로 그의 시는 짜임새가 탄탄하고 주제 의식이 뚜렷이 부각되어 있다.

3. 생명의 존엄성

정춘근 시인이 그려내고자 하는 또 하나의 핵심 사상은 역사적 사실을 근간으로 거기에 존재하는 생명의 존엄성을 발견해 내는 것이다. 그 생명의 존엄성은 생명을 가진 모든 것은 존귀해야 할 가치를 지니고 있다는 인식이 그의 시 전

반에 흐르고 있다. 또한 인간이 인간으로서 누려야 할 권리를 시 속에 함의하고 있는 점 또한 정춘근 시의 우월성이다. 이런 생명의 존엄성, 인간의 권리를 회복하기 위한 내면의식이 이 시집의 모티브로 설정되어 있다. 이런 모티브를 근간으로 그는 역사의 증언 같은 '언어의 집'을 세우고 있는 것이다.

살점이 너덜너덜하고/피가 철철 흐르는 다리를/허리끈을 풀어 조여 매고/군부대 지프차에 실려 가면서/

사람들을 바라보던 그 간절한 눈빛 〈대마리24- 첫 지뢰사고〉5연

"허리끈을 풀어"다친 다리를"조여 매고/군부대 지프차에 실려 가면서/ 사람들을 바라보던 간절한 눈빛"에서 우리는 전율하고 만다. 그 '눈빛'은 곧 생과 사의 갈림길에 선, 죽음의 공포다. 스크린 영상을 마주하듯 생과 사의 검은 이미지가 '대마리' 평야를 휩쓸고 지나간다.

첫 지뢰 사고가 난 밤/한숨을 푹푹 내쉬던/여주에서 온 두 형제가 보따리를 쌌다 〈대마리25-개간을 포기하고 떠난 사람들〉3연

정춘근의 인간에 대한 애착과 존엄성은 그의 생명 의식으로 나타난다. "다리병신"이 되는 것보다는 차라리 구차한 생

이라도 목숨이 더 소중하다고 인식하고 "여주에서 온 두 형제가" 전략촌을 떠나는 것에 초점을 맞춘다. 그의 생명 존엄성의 인식은 여기서 그치는 것이 아니다. "발목이 끊어진 사고 치료비/개인이 알아서 부담"하라는 "신체 포기 각서보다 더 무서웠던/생명 포기 각서 때문이었다"고 (「대마리26-지뢰사고보상금 0원」)에서 진술한다.

이렇게 화자는 생명 사상의 존엄성을 그 이면에 함의하고 있어 한층 생명의 존귀함이 강조된다. 그러나 개척민들을 부리는 관계 기관은 반대로 생명을 티끌같이 취급한다. 오로지 노동 착취의 매개물로 여긴다. 작업을 하다 잘못되면 가차 없이 버리는 그런 지경의 인권 박탈이다. (「대마리29」)에 나타난-"사망 사고"처리의 일면에서 더욱 극명하게 나타난다.

"가마니로 시신을 수습해서/막사로 돌아 왔지만/외지 사람이라/식구들이 올 때까지/텐트 밖에다 모셔 놓고/저녁 식사로/털레기 국수를 끓인다" 그 와중에도 산 사람은 먹어야 하는 것이다. 이렇게 생生과 사死의 대비가 극명하게 드러나고 있다. 죽음 앞에서도 한쪽에서는 살기 위해 "털레기 국수를 끓인다" 아니 끓어야만 하는 생명체의 본능이다. 이런 생명에 대한 애착은「대마리30-보리 두 말」과「대마리46-고라니 새끼」등에서도 잘 나타나고 있다.

4.「대마리」의 문학성

'대마리'는 한정된 공간이다. 그 공간을 배경으로 이렇게 방대한 작품을 구상하여 창작해 냈다는 점에서 우선 정춘근 시인의 시적 재능의 우월성이 평가된다. 70여 편이 넘는 작품마다 구성의 전(轉)과 결연(結聯)에서 극적인 반전으로 작자의 사상과 정서를 잘 살려내고 있다. 이것이 바로 그의 시가 작품으로서의 가치를 높이고 있는 시 정신이다. 모든 예술은 정서적 충돌을 모티브로 하고 있다. 그의 정서는 (「대마리13」) 에서 이렇게 묘사되고 있다.

"갈대가 몸을 비비는 소리가/마치 누군가 다가오는 발자국 같아/화들짝 놀라 눈을 뜨면/가설 텐트 밖을 살금살금 맴도는/바람 소리에 잠을 잘 수가 없었다"라고 감각적 이미지로 승화시킨다. (「대마리12」)에서도 "텐트 밖을 나서/남쪽 하늘을 보면/걱정으로 지샐 여편네와/철 모르는 자식들 초롱초롱한 눈망울이/아픈 별처럼 내려와/눈시울을 젖게 한다"라는 비유로 시적 묘사로 그 이미지를 살려내고 있다. 이밖에도「대마리11-착공식」에서의 장면 묘사,「대마리75-개척비」,「대마리64-적산지」,「대마리24-첫 지뢰사고」,「대마리45-진달래꽃 아래서」,등의 작품은 깊은 울림의 정서를 바탕으로 모더니틱한 감각을 잘 살려내고 있다. 그리고 그는 절규하듯「대마리75(최종)」을 이렇게 장식한다.

6천 평의 약속을 외면했던/대한민국의 거짓말을/ 덮을

수는 없다//지뢰에 끊어진 발목에서/흐르는 뜨거운 피를 움켜쥐고/병원으로 가는 지프차가 오기를 기다리던/핏방울 맺힌 눈동자를/대마리 하늘과 들판은/똑똑히 기억할 것이다 〈대마리75(최종)-개척비〉5.6연

5.시인에 대한 기대

우리는 이번 정춘근의 이 시집에서 문학이란 무엇인가? 그리고 역사란 무엇인가?를 생각하게 된다. 또한 역사의 현장을 그려낸 시를 통하여 우리 민족의 질곡한 역사를 새삼 깨닫게 된다. 그리고 우리가, 우리 서민들의 인권과 권리는 어떤 것이어야 하는가를 생각하게 된다. 또한 정춘근의 작품을 통하여 삶이란 무엇이고 생명이란 무엇인가를 되돌아보게 한다. 이렇게 많은 사유와 인식의 알레고리 망(網)을 던져 놓은 것이 이번 정춘근의 일곱 번째 시집『지뢰꽃 마을 대마리』다.

싸르트르는 말한다. "문학이란 인생에 대한 질문"이라고. 그 질문은 우리의 역사처럼 우리들이 도달할 수 없는 미완성으로 남을 것이다. 왜냐하면 인생에 대한 정답이 없듯이 역사는 계속 흐르고 있기 때문이다. 그리고 역사의 답은 무엇일까? 감히 필자는 여기 정춘근 시인의 시를 통하여 '현장성의 기록'이라고 정의한다. 그 기록은 사실을 바탕으로 하기 때문에 지나친 상상력도, 상징성도, 소설 같은 허구성도 필요가 없다. 그래서 정춘근의『지뢰꽃 마을 대마리』는 더욱

생생한 현장감으로 각인된다.

그리고 그 역사속의 주인공은 누구인가? 어느 시대, 어느 나라든 그 주체는 '민중'이다. 이 시집 『지뢰꽃 마을 대마리』도 민중들의 곡진한 역사다. 아니, 생과 사의 경계를 담보로 하는 생명의 처절한 몸부림이다. 지금도 그 민중들은 철원 땅 '대마리'를 지키고 있다. 그러므로 한 국가를 세우고 지키고 허무는 것도 '민중'이다. 민중은 한 나라의 뿌리다. 뿌리는 곧 역사다.

정춘근 시인은 앞으로도 역사 의식을 지닌 시를 계속 쓸 것이다. 그는 역사의 현장에서 태어나고 자라고 그리고 지금도 그 현장에 살고 있기 때문이다. 대한민국에서 하나밖에 없는 역사적 현장과 고증의 시인으로 거듭 태어날 것을 기대한다.(e)

옮긴 이의 말 Translator's Notes

'지뢰꽃 마을 대마리' 번역은 30명의 서울대학교 자유전공학부 학생들과 전문 위원이 힘을 합쳐 완성한 소설번역 프로젝트였습니다. 해외에서 오래 생활한 글로벌 인재 특별전형 학생들이나 영문학 전공자 정도만 참여하지 않을까 했었던 예상을 보기 좋게 깨고, 자유전공학부에 있는 정말 다양한 전공의 학생들이 참여 의사를 밝혀왔습니다. 휴학생도, 이미 졸업한 학생도, 심지어 군복무 중인 학생도 있었습니다. 모두 한국의 역사와 문학에 많은 관심을 가지고 있었고, 이것을 영어로 번역하는 작업이 의미 있고 필요한 일이라는 것에 동의하고 있었습니다.

분단의 현실을 보여주고 '평화'를 느끼게 하겠다는 관광 상품들이 많습니다. 하지만 젊은 세대들은 오히려 혼란스러워 합니다. 와닿지 않고, 잘 모르겠다는 그들에게 '너희는 우리 역사에 너무 관심이 없다'고 하기엔, 자유전공학부 학생들이 이번 소설번역 프로젝트에 보여준 열의가 대단합니다. 어쩌면 우리 사회는 전쟁, 분단, 평화를 이야기하는 방법을 잘못 알고 있었던 것은 아닐까 싶습니다.

자유전공 부 학생들은 본격적인 번역 작업에 들어가기 전,

세 번의 스터디 모임을 가졌습니다. 단지 번역을 위한 번역이 아닌, 작품과 작가에 대한 깊은 이해를 바탕으로 진정성 있는 결과물을 만들고 싶었습니다. 학생들은 문학 번역 시 고려해야 할 점들에 대해서도 의견을 나누었습니다. 그리고 나름의 원칙을 세웠습니다. 본인의 이해와 느낌에 충실하게 번역하기, 영어권 독자들에게 한국 역사와 문화를 효과적으로 전달하기, 마지막으로 한국 시로서의 정체성을 유지하기.

잘 알려지지 않은 역사의 단면을 담담하면서도 날카롭게 기록한 지역 문인의 작품, 그리고 그것을 영어로 번역해서 더 많은 사람들에게 알리고자 하는 이번 프로젝트는 긴긴 장마와 전염병으로 우울했던 2020년의 여름을 뿌듯한 마음으로 채워준 것 같습니다. '대마리' 시집이 분단 극복과 평화 교육의 새로운 초석이 되는 데 우리의 번역이 미약하게나마 기여할 수 있기를 바랍니다.

The translation of Daemari was the social translating project by 30 students and student program coordinator from College of Liberal Studies(CLS), Seoul National University. Against expectation that only students who gain international admission or students majoring in English would apply for the project, various majors showed willingness to participate without hesitating. Student who is taking the semester off, who already graduated, and even who in the military service was with us. All of them were interested in Korean history and literature, agreeing that translating those to English is very meaningful and necessary.

There are many tour programs in Korea to introduce the reality of the division and to make people feel "peace". But young people are saying it is rather confusing. To them who say "it's not touching our heart" or "It's difficult to understand", blaming that "your generation is too unconcerned with our history" is not appropriate, according to the very impressive passion the students of CLS show to this project. Maybe our society has been misunderstanding how to talk about war, division, and peace.

The students of CLS had group study meetings three times before starting the main work. We wanted to translate with sincerity based on a deep understanding of the original poems and the writer. We also discussed what to consider when translating and established three our own principles: to translate faithfully to our understanding and feeling, to deliver the history and culture of Korea effectively to the English-speaking readers, to maintain the identity of the poems as Korean literature.

The local literature recording the local unknown history

plainly but critically and this translating project to let more people to be aware of this history, filled our heart with pleasure in this depressed summer of long long monsoon and pandemic in 2020. We hope this translation will be a humble help for this Daemari anthology to become a new guide to overcome the division and educate the value of peace.

서울대학교 자유전공학부 College of Liberal Studies, Seoul National University

김지나 전문위원 Kim Jina, Student Program Coordinator

권가영 Kwon Gayoung, 권정유 Kwon Jungyu, 김민서 Kim Minseo, 김연정 Kim Yeonjeong, 김정민 Kim Jungmin, 박서원 Park Seowon, 박연수 Park Yeonsoo, 신임찬 Shin Im-chan, 여윤정 Yeo Yoonjeong, 오하나 Oh Hana, 윤가은 Yun Gaeun, 윤하연 Yoon Hayeon, 윤혜린 Yun Hyerin, 이서영 Lee Seoyoung, 이승주 Lee Seungju, 이윤진 Lee Yunjin, 이재윤 Lee Jaeyoon, 이해원 Lee Haewon, 임혜지 Lim Hyeji, 장민혁 Jang Min Hyuk, 전지우 Jeon Jiwoo, 정영훈 Jeong Younghoon, 정지원 Chung Jiwon, 정해은 Jung Haeeun, 조유진 Cho Yujin, 조하연 Cho Hayun, 조현주 Cho Hyunjoo, 최지윤 Choi Jiyoon, 홍지인 Hong Jiin

시인의 말

열다섯 살 봄이었던가.

우리 집에서 자취하던 친구가 자신이 살고 있는 대마리 이야기를 들려줬었다. 지뢰 사고로 다리 잘린 아버지, 그리고 철책이 없어서 북한 병사가 내려온다는 곳, 해가 떨어지면 검문소에 갇힌 육지 안에 섬 같은 땅의 이야기를 들으며 내가 작가가 된다면 세상에 꼭 남기고 싶다는 다짐을 했었다. 어줍지 않게 시인이 된 다음에도 마음의 빚으로 남았던 대마리를 시집으로 출판할 수 있어서 묵은 숙제를 푼 것 같다.

실천문학사는 내게 고향과 같은 곳이다. 1999년 봄, 시인의 문을 열어 주었고 지금 다시 시집 출판의 기회를 준 것에 감사와 책임감을 느낀다. 특히 윤한룡 대표의 넉넉한 배려에 고개가 절로 숙어진다.

2020년 11월

철원에서 정춘근

실천문학시인선 43

지뢰꽃 마을 대마리

Daemari, The Village of Landmine Flower

2020년 11월 30일 1판 1쇄 인쇄
2020년 11월 30일 1판 1쇄 펴냄

지은이 정춘근
펴낸이 윤한룡
편집 신한선
디자인 윤려하
관리·영업 이소연

펴낸곳 (주)실천문학
등록 10-1221호(1995.10.26)
주소 남양주시 퇴계원읍 퇴계원로 52 405호
전화 02-322-2161~3
팩스 02-322-2166
홈페이지 www.silcheon.com

ISBN 978-89-392-3062-0 03810

본 시집은 강원도와 강원문화재단의 지원을 받아 제작되었습니다.